A ROCK TO STAND ON

Letters From the Past Series

TINA CLOUGH

A ROCK TO STAND ON

Copyright © Tina Clough 2022

The author asserts her moral right to be identified as the author of this work.

PAPERBACK ISBN 978-1-99-118712-3

Lightpool Publishing

www.lightpoolpublishing.com

Cover and book design by Andrene Low

Chapter 1

The chaotic sounds of metal crashing into concrete and glass shattering stopped abruptly, and there was a short moment of total silence, as if the world held its breath, then running footsteps and agitated voices filled the void.

Arapera lay perfectly still, terrified to move, and tried to understand what had happened, how she had got to where she was now. Very close above her face was the side of a car, a shiny blue surface with dents and deep gouges in the paintwork. A woman was calling "help me, help me!" and Arapera could nearly feel her body resting on the inside of the door just inches above her face. She raised a trembling hand to touch it before a hideous vision of her touch making it fall made her pull her hand back. Her elbow hit the pavement hard, she flinched, and a voice right next to her head said, 'Are you injured?'

She turned her head to the side and saw a man's face, calm grey eyes studying her, and realised that he was lying or kneeling with the side of his face resting on the pavement.

'I don't think so – wait a moment.' Carefully she moved her shoulders and legs and found that one foot was caught on something, but otherwise everything felt normal. 'I think I'm OK, thanks - but my left foot is caught. Is the car going to fall? What's holding it up?'

'It skidded on its side up over the pavement and hit a raised concrete ledge – about knee high, so the front of the car is supported by the ledge. If you're not bleeding, I think the best thing is probably to stay where you are until the emergency services arrive.'

He sounded casual and unworried, as if they were discussing something non-threatening and harmless, turning the situation into a mundane event that could happen to anyone, and not until much later did she appreciated how steadying this was for her, how it removed the urgency and made her feel calm too. She felt her customary façade of self-control slide back into place and her breathing slowed. The sound of distant sirens coming closer hardly registered in Arapera's mind, as she tried to piece together what she could recall of the moments before the car came sliding towards her, and then a terrifying thought struck her.

'The girls!' she cried out. 'Oh no, those little girls, where are they? Did the car hit them? Are they OK?'

'I don't know,' said the man, who was still lying

beside the car looking in at her. 'I didn't see any girls. There are two people inside the car, so I'd better get up and tell people there's somebody *under* the car - I'm not sure is anyone else has realised. I don't want them to try to get those people out yet. I'll be back in a moment. And by the way, my name is Liam.'

He doesn't want to spell it out, thought Arapera, but if people start climbing on the car it could fall. I hope he can stop them. A pair of truncated lower legs appeared behind Liam's head, someone said something, and he got to up. She heard him talking and then a loud voice called out for people to stand back from the car and not touch it.

Looking up at the car door so close to her face was disturbing, so Arapera kept her head turned to the right, towards the bright midday sunshine, and waited. All through the ensuing chaos of more sirens approaching, voices giving instructions and rescue personnel looking in to check on her, the man with grey eyes stayed beside the car, and when he was not lying on the ground, she could see his feet just beside her head. Every now and then he lay down again and talked to her. 'What's your name?' he said on one of his little visits.

'Arapera Woodhill.'

'What a pretty name – I've never met an Arapera before.'

'It was my grandmother's name, and her mother's name before her. Then it skipped a generation - they didn't call my mother Arapera, perhaps they thought it was old-fashioned.'

They've appointed him as a liaison person, thought Arapera, I could hear someone telling him that something would take some time, and then he knelt and told me to be patient. And now he's talking to someone again, but I can't hear what they're saying.

'Hey there, still OK?' He was back with the side of his face on the pavement, looking in at her. 'They're going to use props and jacks to stabilize the car before they get anyone out, so I'm afraid you'll have to wait a little longer. How's that foot feeling?'

Just then her phone started making a manic laugh, and she looked down along her side as far as she could without raising her head in the very restricted space, and there was her shoulder bag, level with her knee where the wedge-shaped space under the car was very low. It looked as if it was free but too far from her to reach without squirming, and there was no room to twist her body.

'Oh, bugger!' she said quietly. 'That's dad, I was meeting him for lunch, and he'll wonder where I am.'

Considering that the stability of the car might be precarious, she decided that staying very still was a good idea and tried to ignore the laughing phone. But Liam changed position and managed to reach the bag while the phone continued its noisy alert signal, and she watched him pull it towards him just as it stopped. He got to his feet, but he was back on the ground in a moment with the now silent phone in his hand.

'Here you are - have you got it? Would it be easier if I hold it, and you use your free hand if you want to do something? Or I could call them back for you.'

Her right arm, the one closest to Liam was the only part she could move relatively freely. Her left arm was undamaged but useless because there wasn't enough room for her to move it across her body. Once she had the phone in her hand, she shifted it carefully until her fingers held it firmly and used her thumb to operate it. One missed call and a text message from her father. She pressed the Call button and managed to twist her arm enough to hold the phone to her ear, telling herself to sound calm and not give anything away, to avoid him getting the impression he should come and support her.

'Hi Dad, I won't be able to make it for lunch, sorry! I should have called sooner, I was on my way, but there was an accident right in front of me and I'm a witness, so I have to stay here for a while. It's a bit chaotic and I'll have to wait till they have time to talk to me. I'll see you next time you're in town.'

She listened for a few moments while Liam stayed where he was, lying flat on the ground with his hand on her bag just beside her shoulder.

'Of course, I don't expect you to hang around, you go back to work. OK, dad – see you!' Turning the phone off she handed it to him and watched him slide it into her bag.

'Well, aren't you a cool customer?' he said appreciatively. 'Not many would have had the presence of mind to think of *that* – I suppose you didn't want your dad to come rushing here in a panic.'

'God no!' The thought nearly made her laugh, which was a bizarre impulse in the middle of such a fraught situation. Her father would make everything worse and very likely kneel on the pavement to pray and attract an even bigger crowd than what she imagined was there already. He would be a total embarrassment, but this wasn't something she could tell a stranger, so instead she said, 'This would have made him super anxious - and he'd drive me crazy. I'd rather lie here in peace and quiet without any drama and tell him later – if I have to.'

'Amazing girl!' said Liam and then someone spoke next to him, so he pushed the bag towards her and was replaced by a fireman telling her not to worry about the car rocking a bit and to stay still, they would soon have the car secured so they could lift it off her foot. 'But when we do lift it, I want you to stay where you are – don't try and get out by yourself. We'll get you out carefully - we don't know how badly damaged your trapped foot is, so just be patient for a little longer.'

As Liam lowered himself to the ground again, Arapera managed to manoeuvre the phone out of the bag one-handed, so she could call the office with the same excuse in case it would take some time to get back to work. Theresa in reception said casually, 'Oh, don't worry - Shane's out trying to charm a prospective client, and the boys in your team are playing soccer in the passage and acting like five-year-olds.'

When Arapera limped out of the lift and into the reception area at the office, she was relieved to find that Theresa was not at her desk, though she could hear her voice from further down the hall and only just managed to reach the toilets without anyone seeing her.

In her mind, getting tidied up and regaining the last missing pieces of her normal persona had become paramount during the walk back from the accident scene to the office. Arapera felt certain that her ability to keep the after-effects of the ordeal under control depended on presenting an unconcerned appearance, and not admitting to the acute fear she had only just kept under control. She knew instinctively that revealing any signs of distress might leave her vulnerable, and over-the-top displays of sympathy could let the genie of shock out of the bottle.

That feeling while I was under the car, she thought, when Liam and I kept up a calm and controlled dialogue, as if nothing untoward was happening, it kind of created a barricade against emotional turmoil, and we won the battle, we kept it up and there were no tears and no screams of panic.

Studying her face in the mirror for a moment and marvelling at how deceptive a facial expression can be, she thought of the last couple of hours and a small shiver ran down her back. Luck had truly been on her side; the way the car had settled leaving just enough space for her body, and that Liam happened to be nearby, not only to tell people not to touch the car, but because it was hard to imagine anyone else providing that calm and steadying influence.

Standing there with one hand on the tap and the other reaching for the soap dispenser, she tried a little smile and thought it looked quite natural and reflected none of the emotions tumbling through her mind. The car could have slipped off that ledge at any stage, fallen and crushed her skull or petrol could have leaked out and started a fire, and she shuddered at the images this brought up in her mind. Quickly she washed her hands, brushed her hair and retreated into a cubicle with a handful of wet paper towels. Five minutes later, having reapplied the elastic bandage the ambulance man had given her, she limped into the office she shared with two male co-workers and sank into her chair.

'Long lunch, ha?' said Thomas, whose desk was at right angles to hers and then his face took on an expression of concern. 'Oh, no – your ankle is bandaged, my God – what happened?'

'I tripped and twisted my ankle. I got such a fright - a car came across the pavement right in front of me really fast and then it flipped on its side. And because I was a witness I had to hang around until they had time to talk to me. It was pretty chaotic. *And* I didn't get to have lunch with my dad – *and* I forgot to buy something to eat on the way back. But thank goodness I'm wearing flats, or I wouldn't have been able to walk back, I don't think.'

Their curiosity was rampant, and she was forced to describe the accident in detail, but from the imagined point of view of a bystander, and her explanation of how she limped into a pharmacy and bought an elastic bandage was accepted at face value.

'It's not serious – I'll be fine in a couple of days. Now guys – as team leader I've done just about all I can to convince Shane to apply to the top boss for a budget increase, so we can get that software. I think I've used all the arguments I can possibly think of and the points you two have brought up, but he won't budge. Any new ideas?'

'Did you point out that we know the opposition has it already and they're using it as a selling point? It's mentioned on their website,' said Thomas and reached out to tap the head of the laughing cat figurine stuck to his desk with Blu-tack. For a minute its high-pitched giggle was the only sound in the office, while they glanced silently from one to the other, reluctance written clearly on their faces.

'He's got to do it!' said Thomas forcefully. 'This is bloody ridiculous! We can't delay it any longer, it's getting urgent and soon everyone else in the industry will have it and we'll be left behind. It would save time and time is money, but you used that argument in your notes to him, didn't you – right at the start?'

'I wonder why he's so against it,' said Bugsy slowly, as if this thought had just occurred to him, when the others had wondered the same thing for weeks. 'We've told him in detail why we need it, and all the benefits - and he still drags his feet about making a decision. It's only a twelve hundred a month or something for the version I think we should have – not the end of the world.'

Arapera shook her head, frustrated and out of ideas. 'It's either because he hates change, or he hates making decisions. Whichever it is, he isn't the right fit to manage this section – and please don't quote me outside this room. I've talked to the other teams, and they say if we get it, we can integrate the app team's work with ours and link it to the online and text promos we do for the supermarkets, seamless and non-repetitive. Lots of time savings all round. But Shane's unable to look forward and see that we need to get this now or we'll be outsmarted by the competition.'

She lifted her left foot to rest it on her wastepaper basket and suppressed a groan when her ankle protested, put it back on the floor and continued. 'It's a shame the other team leaders have this self-protective thing going about not wanting to attract the notice of the CEO. I've got a feeling they think Shane will mention their names if they support me openly. Everyone's scared of Blair.'

Thomas swivelled his chair two full revolutions very fast, put his foot against Arapera's desk to stop himself and grinned. 'Except you – everyone except you. How come? Were you born brave, or did you have to learn it?'

'Don't be silly, Thomas! I find Blair as intimidating as everyone else – and for women it's worse, we trigger his most extreme power and control response with a dose of condescension as icing on the cake.'

She frowned at Bugsy, who was absentmindedly picking at a red spot on his chin, and he dropped his hand. 'I think Shane prides himself on saving the big boss money, it's like he thinks it's the reason he's been made section manager, he's a spending filter. And I can't go over his head to top management – it could be seen as subversive.' She grinned at their disgruntled faces. 'Not that I mind being subversive in a good cause, but you know what this place is like, very hierarchical.'

Chapter 3

When Arapera let herself into the flat that night, Carter was busy at the kitchen bench, but her limping footsteps alerted him. 'What happened to you? What's wrong with your ankle?'

He put down the knife and the half onion he was holding and came around the table to where she had sunk down on the sofa, feeling exhausted.

'You're looking tired. Let me look at that ankle, no don't move, just stay where you are.'

'I'm fine – it's nothing worth worrying about. I just tripped when I was rushing to meet dad for lunch, so I wrapped it up to get some sympathy from the boys.'

Ignoring her protests Carter knelt on the floor and started unwinding the crepe bandage. 'Who is the nurse here? Is it you or me? I'll just have a look. I know you won the stoic-of-the-year award when you were three, but – ah, yes - look at that.'

He ran his fingers over the swelling on the outside of her ankle, moved her foot slightly from side to side, prodded gently and looked up, blue eyes crinkling at the corners.

'I think you'll live. You've sprained the lateral ligament. Not too badly - if it happened at lunchtime and the swelling isn't any worse than this, you'll probably be fine in a few days. It's a bit late for ice, but we'll get some anti-inflammatory gel on it and wrap it up properly, so it's held firmly – you'll be much more comfortable.'

He got to his feet and disappeared while Arapera remained slumped on the sofa, internally debating with herself about how much she would tell Carter. She had thought about this all the way home, limping to the bus stop and sitting distracted on the nearly full bus until she got off at Palmer Street for the final, painfully slow walk to the flat. Perhaps just a scaled-down version without the whole drama and no mention of jacks and props and how the car kept rocking ever so slightly while she lay there helpless, listening to the creaking of stressed metal. She realised that for the first time since she met Carter in high school, she was preparing herself not to be totally honest with him.

I'm not dishonest, she told herself, but I'm not ready to relive that scene again just yet, I might lose control. I'll keep it minimal, but I'll tell him the basics.

Ten minutes later Arapera's foot was resting on a wine carton, which turned out to be the perfect height, she had a glass of wine in her hand and Carter moved the bowl of salted peanuts to where she could reach it.

'Wine at both ends, the perfect life, eh? Now tell me the truth, girl – I saw that hesitation when you said you "just tripped" so there's more to it, isn't there? Remember that I know what I'm talking about after being in a relationship with the world's worst and most frequent liar for two years before I dumped him - I'm an expert at detecting evasions and half-truths.' He sat down and sent a determined look at her across the coffee table; the look that usually meant, "now, would you please be serious and listen to me."

She nodded, took a sip of wine and smiled fondly at him, knowing she must tell him after all. He was the only person in her life she always told everything, and it didn't matter that she might feel overwhelmed reliving the drama of the crash

'I know – of course I'll tell you, no need to remind me of the rules.'

She paused for a moment and decided to start out by telling it straight and minimal just to see his reaction. 'I somehow ended up under a car that turned on its side on the pavement right in front of me.'

The expression on his face made her laugh, which in turn made him even more suspicious, as she had known it would.

'You what?! Under a car on its side and all you got was a sprained ankle? No way! Now - would you please be serious and tell me what really happened.'

Somehow her concise and slightly flippant description of the event made her feel less stressed, and now she could continue in the same vein, making the drama less traumatic than it had been.

'It *is* true, I swear it is. Like a minor miracle really, now that I think of how it sounds - I could have been seriously hurt, or even killed, but I was lucky. It was the most incredible thing.'

She took a sip of wine and considered how best to describe it. Carter's serious eyes were fixed on hers and he was leaning forward slightly, as if he expected her to be evasive or not telling the truth.

She must try to make him see it through her eyes. 'You'll have to try to picture this like a film clip in your head. There I was, walking along Lambton Quay on my way to have lunch with dad, and a car swerved diagonally across the street, accelerating like crazy towards me - and then it mounted the pavement, kind of leapt across the kerb - the driver must have had a medical event or something. Or maybe they panicked or turned the wheel very suddenly, because when it hit the edge of the pavement it started tipping sideways, toward me.'

'OK - so how did you get *under* it?' Carter still looked dubious, as if he wasn't sure what to think. 'I mean, you're standing up one second and then you're lying flat on the ground?'

'It fell over, Carter! On its side – and it slid as it fell until the nose hit this concrete ledge thing, and the car lifted on to it somehow and came to rest like that – with the front of the car lifted up. And I was lying on my back in a wedge-shaped space with the passenger door just above my nose and from there the space got lower until it kind of ran out more or less at my feet.'

Carter's eyes were still unblinkingly fixed on hers and she could see he was fascinated. 'And?'

'What do you mean – and?'

'I mean, how the hell did you get there? If the car slid on its side until it hit that ledge you would have been crushed if you got in the way, so it must have tilted gradually as it went across the footpath, mustn't it?'

Arapera thought back and tried to picture how it happened, but she could only make assumptions, because she had no clear recollection of exactly how she had ended up under the car.

'It did tip gradually - I remember an ultra-fast reaction, thinking "Will it right itself or tip over?" But I can't remember exactly how I got under it. And please don't look at me like that! I don't remember falling, so I truly can't say for sure, but I think I know *why* I ended up on the ground. There were these two little girls in front of me and to one side, to the left, just a step ahead of me - and I was sure the car would hit the three of us. You now, like a split-second thing that flashed into my mind, so I did my famous netball side-step that I haven't used for years and kind of threw myself across in front of them trying to push them back, away from the car.'

She stopped talking and sat looking down into her wineglass, confused and irritated. Now that she was trying to describe it, she could hear that it seemed not only unlikely, but completely mad.

'God, it's so confusing!' she burst out, frustrated and suddenly on the verge of tears. 'I *can't* tell you exactly because I don't *know* – it happened so damn fast. And I must have manged to push those girls aside, but doing that was probably what made me fall, and the car must have kind of folded on its side over me – all at the same time. Perhaps that's how the nose of the car got up on the little ledge, it didn't push up onto it – it came down onto it. And my foot twisted sideways and was stuck.'

Carter nodded, satisfied that this made sense and he could understand what had happened. He's always like this, thought Arapera and watched his eyes gazing unseeing at the wall behind her, he always needs to get a firm grip on the facts and make sure he knows how things hang together.

'And they weren't injured, those girls? So, you saved them?'

'I don't know – there was a guy there who lay down on the pavement and talked to me and kept me sane until they got me out, and he said there weren't any girls, but I thought he probably hadn't noticed. You know, he spotted me under the car and didn't really look around. So, when I finally got out, I asked first the ambulance guys and then a cop who came to talk to me. And they all said no girls had been hurt and nobody else had mentioned them, so they must have just run off.'

They looked at each other for a long silent moment, then Carter moved his head slowly from side to side in disbelief at how fortunate she had been. 'You were *so* lucky! Possibly millimetres away from being crushed or mangled – I shudder to think what could have happened to you. A lot more than a twisted ankle, for sure. And you're probably right, those girls got such a fright they just ran away in a panic.'

Arapera nodded. 'I think so - they were quite young, perhaps eight or nine, something like that. Maybe their mum took them to town, and they were just dawdling along behind her. I bet she got a fright when they told her what happened.'

Carter went back to the kitchen bench, saying casually over his shoulder, 'Are you going to tell Dan?'

This was the first time either of them had mentioned Dan's name since she told Carter a couple of days ago that she had broken up with him. Arapera knew Carter was giving her a chance to think before she replied, because he still didn't know why she suddenly broke it off with Dan, and he was probably hoping they would patch it up. After an initial period of suspicion from Dan's side and some reluctance on Carter's, they became friends when they discovered they both loved playing chess, a skill Arapera had no wish to acquire to please either of them. A couple of weeks ago, Dan's firm sent him to Dunedin to manage their big furniture store there when the manager was killed in a car crash, and though it was only a couple of days since Arapera told Carter that she had broken up with Dan, she had actually done it the day before he left Wellington.

'But why?' asked Carter when she finally told him. 'What is it you're not telling me? You say, "I broke up with him two weeks ago" and then you don't tell me why. You always tell me things – what's so bad that you can't say it?'

But all she did at the time was shake her head and pick up her phone to avoid his eyes. She knew he was still looking at her, but she ignored him. The truth was so humiliating and hurtful, that she couldn't bear to say it out loud, not even to Carter, or not yet anyway. Something of her inner conflict must have shown on her face because he walked around the back of her chair, leaned down and kissed the top of her head. 'Never mind, girl – you don't have to tell me.'

Now he turned to look at her, their eyes met, and she shook her head. 'No, I'm not telling him. There is no reason for him to know. He's not part of my life and I'll never have anything to do with him again.'

· · ·

Carter, who was on his last week of night shifts in ED, left at half past ten to catch a ride to the hospital with another nurse and Arapera remained on the sofa, feeling drained and slightly worried. Somehow, the fact that she couldn't picture in her mind exactly how she had ended up under that car was slowly eroding her façade of composure. In her mind, she recreated that frantic side-step and the way she flung her body diagonally in front of the girls, shoving them back with her out-stretched left arm, but between that split-second movement and finding herself under the car her mind was a blank.

Did the force of that shove, the resistance of her arm hitting the girls, create enough momentum to topple her in the other direction, falling neatly flat just as the car settled over her? Why had those few seconds been wiped from her mind? Frustrated she got to her feet and let out a little groan of pain when she put weight on her left foot. Limping to the bench to top up her glass of water, she swung her left arm out horizontally and tried to imagine the feeling of her arm coming into contact with the girls, and how that movement would have sent them sprawling to one side and her falling to the other, but it didn't seem real. It was just a theoretical explanation, there was no remnant in her memory of the physical touch of her arm slamming into them. It worried her intensely and an hour later, after trying to read and giving it up as hopeless while her mind kept replaying the accident scene, she took two painkillers and went to bed, convinced that she would never fall asleep.

Lying in the half dark of her bedroom with the quilt pulled up into a tent shape to avoid the weight of it on her left foot, she wished she could talk to Liam again because he might have seen it happen. And even if he hadn't seen it, he would discuss it in that dark, confident voice and make it seem reasonable that she couldn't remember it herself. Such a talent, she thought, to be able to inject complete calm into a situation like that, and make her feel that she was perfectly safe, that everything would be all right.

Chapter 4

The **Soldierpilotpilot Blog** (262418 followers)

#coolchick

The ultimate definition of coolness is the headline for today, or it would be if I used headlines. The debate about rising sea levels and our moral obligation to take in populations from low lying Pacific Islands (or not) will have to wait a day or two, because this story needs to be told.

So today we will talk about being cool, super cool. You might prefer to call it presence of mind or composure or simply being brave, but whatever your choice of word, I now have the yardstick that all future claims of coolness will be measured against (and probably fail).

Here's the story: Today at lunch time I was walking down Lambton Quay (Wellington) on my way to meet a friend for lunch (one of my rare trips to the city), when a car veered across the street, tried to correct its course and, suddenly accelerating hard instead of braking, mounted the pavement (still accelerating), and after an almighty crash, came to rest on its side with the nose of the car lifted off the ground by a knee-high concrete ledge at the inner edge of the pavement.

People rushed in to help, but it seems I was the only one who noticed the young woman under the car. She was lying on her back with her nose barely a hand's breadth below the front passenger door above her head, and the rest of her body just fitted in the wedge-shaped space that disappeared to nothing about level with her feet.

Here's where ultimate cool comes in - try to picture the scene in your mind when you read this. When the screech of metal graunching along concrete and the tinkling of shattered glass ceases, I get down on the ground, and by putting my cheek on the paving and looking in sideways see a calm face looking back. No particular expression of fear or worry, and seemingly not a hair out of place — a long strand of dark hair neatly curling on her shoulder. When I ask if she is injured or bleeding, she thanks me politely and says that she thinks she is OK, but her left foot is caught on something. And then her expression turns frantic, and she exclaims, 'Oh no! Those little girls! Are they OK?'

I tell her I didn't see any little girls, and we agree they probably just ran off in a fright. When her phone emits a crazy laugh alert inside her bag, which is out of her reach by her knees, she twists her neck to look, realises she can't possibly reach it and says quietly, 'Oh bugger, that's my dad, he'll be wondering where I am'.

I manage to reach the bag and pull her phone out, but now the call is dead. I pass her the phone (her right arm is free to move) and she manages to call back while I shamelessly listen to the most accomplished and reasonable-sounding string of blatant lies I have ever heard. She tells her father that she is a witness at an accident scene and won't make it to lunch because, "they want to talk to me, but it's pretty chaotic here and I have to wait my turn."

All the while the noise of sirens approaching, people shouting instructions and the occasional groan from stressed metal continues around us.

And *THEN*, and listen carefully now people, then she turns to me and explains that she doesn't want her dad to come rushing because he would drive her crazy and she would rather lie there "in peace and quiet and wait".

And while I digest this amazing statement, still lying on my side looking in under the car (and *BTW*, also acting as a liaison person with the rescue personnel) she makes another call. This time to her office, and she makes the same excuse for possibly being late back from lunch, laughs (yes, really — she laughs) at something the person at the other end tells her and says, "tell them to behave themselves", and then she goes back to lying there looking totally composed.

She remains utterly calm for the next forty minutes or so, while emergency services work on stabilising the car with jacks and props. When they finally lift it a bit, pull her out and help her to her feet, she finds that her left ankle is very sore (evident from a brief, agonised facial expression, but not a single moan or yelp was heard). She refuses to be led to an ambulance and asks if she can please have an elastic bandage. After a brief, but firm negotiation the ambulance guy gives in and hands her the bandage *to apply herself, she sits down on the kerb, winds it tight around her ankle, gets to her feet and walks away limping. I stay on the side lines prepared to intervene, if necessary, but no help is needed.*

I have never seen anything so cool in my life, not on active duty during my time in the British army or anywhere else. The entire time I was there, I was tense with apprehension, desperately hoping that the nose of the car wouldn't slide off the ledge and crush her, and with the car settling a centimetre or two a couple of times, I'm sure she was as acutely aware of that risk as I was.

Chapter 5

Two days later Arapera could walk without a limp, but on Carter's insistence she continued to wear the elastic bandage, which he applied each morning.

'It's not that I don't think you could do it right, if you wanted to,' he said, kneeling at her feet, his large, warm hand holding her foot steady. 'It's just that I know you *wouldn't* do it right, because you don't realise it's important – which I do. Perhaps tomorrow we'll leave it off – take it off when you get home tonight and walk around without it, and we'll check if the swelling stays down.'

'Thanks, Carter – you know I love the way you look after me, don't you? I just protest for forms sake, so I won't look like a wuss and ruin my reputation.'

Apart from her younger brother Jackson, she loved Carter more than anyone and that included both her parents and all of her friends. Tragic, she thought, here she was, heading for thirty and she only had two people in her life that she truly loved. She was very fond of her best friend Carmen, of course, but she didn't love her, not with that all-enveloping emotion that real love confers. Carter, on the other hand, was like a constant factor of kindness and affection in her life as he had been from the time they met in high school, when she was thirteen, a steady and supportive presence to turn to when her home life was stressful.

So now she added, just to make sure he really understood what she had never said to him before, 'I really do love you, you know – and I don't know what I'd do without you.'

'I love you too, poppet,' was all he said, but he smiled as he put the safety pin through the bandage and got to his feet.

She cooked dinner that night though it was Carter's week, because doing something with her hands seemed to divert her thoughts from worrying about why she couldn't remember all the details of the accident episode. The blank in her mind continued to nag at her and knowing that she had somehow lost those few seconds took on more importance as time went on.

'It's as if someone has removed a couple of seconds with a scalpel, very precisely,' she told Carter, who was lying on the sofa scrolling through photos on a dating app on his phone. 'And it's not as if I was knocked unconscious or anything, I've not got a lump on the back of my head, so no head injury. So why can't I remember?'

'For heaven's sake, are you still worrying about that?' He looked up and put his phone to one side. 'I didn't realise – it's just one of those things that happens quite a lot when people are in a state of shock. We get people coming into ED who haven't been concussed, they're just temporarily traumatised and shocked, and they say things like "could you ask if they found my bag" – when the bag is right there beside them on the gurney, because they asked the ambulance man to find it and give it to them. It's not worth worrying about and the memory might come back – it will just pop up in your head one day when you least expect it.'

She nodded, because she didn't want him to worry about her obsession and turned back to stir the white cheese sauce with mustard she was making for a dish of baked cauliflower. Obsessing about anything was an unusual thing for her to do, and she wished she could ask Liam exactly what he saw, if he really looked around, or if he perhaps saw the entire thing happening from the start, which would be even better. Even if he didn't see it all from the start, they would discuss it and she was certain that hearing him talk about it would settle the nagging worry in the back of her mind and she would be able to accept that although she had mislaid those couple of seconds it didn't matter.

· · ·

Soldierpilotpilot (279413 followers)

#Coolchick

Once again, a pause in our current discussions about climate change, the real reasons for the fuel price increase and the US Congress debacle, though the latter is admittedly such good TV it might as well have been scripted as a drama series.

Well, folks – that long piece about #coolchick, as she is now known everywhere, not just in this blog, paid dividends for my ego. Not only am I deluged on social media with comments, requests for her name, her age and her workplace. None of which I will respond to, of course, but my entire blog post has been requested by the Sunday Star-Times and will feature in next weekend's edition. I might just change my hashtag to #soldierpilotpilotwriter.

And again, of course I haven't told anyone anything personal about the Queen of Cool - not that I know anything worth telling. Let's respect her privacy and just admire her from afar.

Soldierpilotpilot (282913 followers)

#coolchick

#thequeenofcool

Another day without our usual topics – or maybe this is becoming my usual topic because someone needs to keep on top of this.

It seems quite unfair that after my decision not to name the Queen of Cool (I do know her name, she told me at the time), it's now out there everywhere. And not only her name but also videos taken by bystanders which I was totally unaware of at the time. Yes, I know - I should have known this would happen and that it would only take minutes for those videos to be linked to my blog and then for someone on social media to supply her name.

But really, is this hysterical attention fair to a person, who probably just wants to remain private? Can't you leave her alone? She probably doesn't want to have people trying to take selfies with her or buy her a drink. I'm safe (and I'm not cool, so not such a desirable photo object). I just do my errands, write my blog and occasionally escape out to sea or into the air, where nobody can follow me. But the Queen of Cool (and no, I will not use her name here) has no choice. She has to park her car, or wait for a bus, walk to her office and maybe go out for a coffee at lunchtime — when someone pops up and asks for a selfie or takes a photo and posts it on social media. Shame on you!

I know this whole mess is my fault to some extent, but when I started blogging about her, I never expected things to take this turn. And I do understand the press wanting to interview her after the videos went public, and it's probably partly my fault for raving about her incredible composure and stirring up all this interest in her, but can't the rest of you just leave her alone?

And a brief reply to the correspondent calling him/herself CosmoØ (very clever handle by the way, congratulations). No, the huge and exhaustive discussion many of you had on my various social media pages and on my website regarding my blog post about Boris Johnson: this is not going to be revived, unless he somehow manages to retrieve his reputation and then inevitably destroy it again. And what are the chances of that? Though you're welcome to continue arguing about it without any input from me.

Chapter 6

Arapera had just come out of the shower when Carter called out from the kitchen. 'Your phone is laughing hysterically. Do you want me to pick up?'

'Yes, please – I'm coming.' Arapera stepped into her panties and pulled her top over her head as she walked across the living room. Though she would rather not talk to her father just then, she knew that early morning was perfect because it gave her an iron-clad excuse to keep the conversation short and say she had to go, or she would be late for work.

'Hi, dad! How are you?' Keeping her voice upbeat and cheerful was vital until she knew what he was calling about. The longer she could delay the inevitable, the better for her peace of mind, because she knew that at least one harsh reproach about something was inevitably coming her way, it always did. Carter continued to spread butter on his toast, and she knew he would be hoping this would not turn into another session of criticism and blame, ruining her morning. Right from the start of their teenage friendship he had tried to protect her, because he knew how dangerous her father was.

'He is mentally ill,' Carter had said a couple of weeks ago. 'It's a fact, poppet – no point in denying reality. He has a very lose grip on his temper, he's a fanatic and sees everything in black and white. And someone, who actually believes that God is telling him things that the rest of us don't know, that's a textbook case of delusion.'

The voice in Arapera's ear was strident and impatient and she stood quietly waiting for what was to come, trying to keep her expression neutral, well aware of Carter's heightened awareness.

'I only just heard about that accident! You should have told me at the time – fancy just saying you were a witness when you were lying under a car and in danger! I would have come immediately, and I would have prayed for you – I really do believe that vicinity prayers have a better chance of being heard than the remote kind.'

Her father's voice was taking on a note of suppressed anger. 'And I do hope you asked God to forgive you for only asking for help in emergencies. Your relationship with God really concerns me, Arapera - we need to sit down and have another talk about this! And are you OK?'

She stood silent as he continued, alternating between blaming her for her religious shortcomings and saying he hoped she was all right, though it sounded like an afterthought, not something of particular importance, and he never waited for an answer. This kind of conversation was routine, and her best chance of not getting into an argument with him was to just listen and then divert him. She waited for the right moment and said, 'Did you read the email from auntie Jean? About Rickie and how he loves his new job in Scotland?'

'No, I haven't seen it – when was this?' His voice changed and he sounded genuinely interested, which was exactly what she had hoped for when she decided which diversion to use; Rickie had always been a favourite of his.

'Oh, just this morning, it was addressed to everyone in the family. I haven't finished reading it - it's quite long, so I'll look at it later. He was so lucky to get that job, wasn't he? He's talked about living in Scotland and tracking down all the old family graves since high school – such an oddball!'

'I'm so pleased he got it, I prayed that he would.' Her father sounded smug, as if his intervention had done the trick. 'And don't call him an oddball – that's not kind. He's a very serious boy and he's been interested in family history since he was at primary school.'

'Yeah, I know, but I've got to go, Dad – I've got a meeting first thing, so I have to be at work on time.'

She put the phone back on the bench next to her bag and caught Carter's little smile out of the corner of her eye. 'Yes? Something's funny?'

'That bloody manic laughter you have to warn you it's your dad calling! It makes me jump every time he calls – I hope he never finds out.'

'How could he?' Arapera turned back halfway across the room on her way to finish dressing. 'I wouldn't call him when he's present, so I think it's safe, don't you?' Then she laughed and added. 'But once when he was in town and we went out for lunch, I got a call from Mum and he jumped at the sound of that giggle I have as her call signal, so I just killed it and pretended it was some kind of video alert. He would have drawn all kinds of conclusions from that – he's never stopped saying he should never have married her because she's frivolous and she's hardened her heart against God. He never thinks of it that if he hadn't married her, he wouldn't have me and Jackson – not that he seems to like us very much, at least not me.'

Carter looked pained at the thought of Arapera's father and his religious extremism, knowing how badly it had affected her childhood and their family life, and he usually refused to treat her comments about him lightly. But this time he opted for saying nothing critical, instead he looked her pointedly up and down and then up again.

'And what are you adding to panties and that short little top, may I ask? I hope you're not thinking of that pencil skirt you bought the other day.'

She stared suspiciously at him because Carter did not usually comment on what she was wearing, and the look he gave her must mean something. 'Why? Do you think it's too tight? I *did* ask you when I tried it on, and you said it was fine.'

'Oh no, you look very cute in it, but I know you'll be wearing high heels if you put that skirt on, so would you please change your mind and wear trousers and flats, not heels of any height. That ankle is nearly back to normal, and I don't want you to stuff it up again.'

She snorted, amused and a bit disconcerted that he had it right. She had planned to wear the new pencil skirt and heels, because it was a lovely spring morning, the skirt was new, and she hadn't yet worn it to work. 'You're beginning to act like you're my mother.'

'God no! I don't want to be anyone's mother. I'm just your resident nurse, so do what I say, will you? And I've got a date tonight, a new guy, so not sure what time I'll be back. Supposed to be just for a drink, but it might turn into dinner.'

Chapter 7

The meeting with Shane and the new client was scheduled for half past eight, but the client, Ms Carlson, was running late. Arapera sat quietly at her desk with her headphones on to avoid the boys talking to her and went through what she knew about this potential new client, which wasn't much. All Shane had said was that her business had websites and phone apps that needed work and analysis, and though this was very minor in comparison to most jobs they did, for some reason he seemed very keen to get her custom and had agreed to a meeting instead of just getting the details by email. Desperate to replace the two contracts he lost this month, thought Arapera, even with small jobs.

Hoping that this could turn out to be the perfect occasion to push for the new software in a different way, she rehearsed a variety of remarks she might get a chance to insert into the discussion with Ms Carlson, hoping to make it seem that it had already been agreed to by Shane without actually saying so. It would have to sound like an off the cuff remark, very lowkey, and she must not so much as glance at Shane while she spoke, or he would interrupt. A dialogue with a new client in Shane's presence might be an invaluable way to influence him. Risky, she admitted to herself, but it would be worth it in the long run if it worked, and it could hardly make Shane resent her more than he already did. The fact that she had a degree in computer software engineering had rankled from the moment he accidentally overheard someone tell Arapera that Shane didn't. The incident in the break room where this took place was etched on her mind; Shane in the doorway and she half turned towards him, catching the look on his face. If only she had stood with her back to the door, she thought now, then he would have had a chance to walk away, and the issue would not have become such an obstacle. He probably took the fact that she would defend her side in a discussion without backing down as a sign that she regarded herself as superior. He had no idea, she thought now, that what she did despise him for was how slow he was to grasp facts and reach a conclusion, his indecisiveness.

At quarter to nine they went into the conference room across the passage with the immaculate Ms Carlson, who calmly apologised for being late, said her taxi had not arrived as ordered and turned down the offer of coffee.

To Arapera's surprise the opportunity to trot out her prepared piece about the software appeared very quickly. Ms Carlson had brought a couple of printouts that she passed across the table with the explanation that she had written what she called a one-page amateur's vision of what she would ideally like them to do for her but welcomed more suggestions.

Shane glanced at the page and cast a look in Arapera's direction, his expression indecisive. She noticed the way his eyes flicked back to the document and then back to her and she could imagine his jumbled thoughts. Should he read it right through now? And if he did, would Arapera cover the time gap by chatting to Ms Carlson? Or would Arapera also start reading it and then Ms Carlson would be left sitting there waiting, or should he just hope he got the gist of it from that first glance and start discussing it. Arapera took over as she often had to when Shane would otherwise end up floundering and getting nowhere.

'I think it would give us some clarity if you told us the gist of it first, and then we'll read this later, before we put together a proposal,' she said and put her hand on the paper Ms Carlson had handed her, smiling to take the edge of what might be taken as criticism. 'Just give us an outline now, so we have a starting point for a first discussion.'

Ms Carlson put her elbows on the table, balanced

her slim silver pen perfectly horizontally between the tips of her forefingers and looked at them over it.

'A brief summary would be that I want to have a one-stop place for everything IT – for example, let's say a website or a product needs to change, then I want the page in question and the apps for Androids and iPhones updated or fixed smoothly and fast - and at the same time. And of course, our various online ads and the meta data for search engines should update more or less automatically to the changes made, if that's possible, not as an afterthought and out of step. I want a company that can make these things happen more or less immediately and in a synchronised way. Say we decide to offer a discount on something or a second article for half price or whatever, or a special deal – I want all our online material to be instantly up to date. I know I sound demanding, but she who pays the piper and all that - what might sound inconsequential to you is important to me.'

She quirked an eyebrow at Shane and Arapera, her gaze moving from one to the other. What has she picked up? wondered Arapera. Something about the dynamic between us has alerted her, or was it Shane's body language when I took over? Grasp the iron while it's hot, as Jackson says, I'll take the risk and launch my strategy right away.

'We've actually been talking about some very sophisticated new software just recently,' she said smoothly, trying to sound relaxed and confident. 'It's very clever and it makes the sort of things you describe quick and easy. It will allow us to set up linked modules so all those functions you listed can happen seamlessly. Updated base data feeds from one module to the other and there's no need to write code for new aspects or use different software or log into various social media accounts each time. If you're familiar with Excel, you would perhaps think of the concept as linked spreadsheets with hyperlinks and some add-ons? A bit like Flutter, which you might have heard about, but more powerful - very complex.'

'Yes!' said Ms Carlson and smiled. 'That's exactly the kind of ability to instantly update and change that I want – websites, phone apps and so on, the whole lot and nothing forgotten by mistake, as sometimes happens now -no mismatched information in different media. If you can do it, I would move the webhosting of all my websites to you, including email accounts, of course. Do you have the staff to make changes frequently and fast, as I ask for them – no delays?'

She glanced at Shane, who didn't comment, and continued. 'My businesses are forever developing and expanding, and I need to feel assured I'm always one step ahead, with no lose ends. If you can do it seamlessly as you put it, I would be prepared to sign a contract for all our work to go to you for a fixed period of time as a trial run, say six months. The company I've used until now disappointed me – they aren't flexible enough and I don't like waiting for results or have things happen in an unsynchronised way.'

Her gaze moved between Shane and Arapera, treating them politely as equals, but Arapera sensed that the focus was on her, and she could imagine how conflicted Shane felt. She knew he'd probably like to take her out of the room and tell her she was out of order, and that he wasn't prepared to ask for the money to buy new and expensive software, but he also wanted this contract after losing two clients in the last few weeks, one of them a big one.

'Businesses?' she asked before Shane got his thoughts into order. 'More than one?'

'Five so far,' said Ms Carlson coolly and smiled briefly. 'I'm working on number six and seven, which will also need their own websites and total media set-ups before they launch. All my businesses are distinct entities in all respects − legally and financially, and they have different names and their own websites, separate email addresses and so on. I run them myself, but I haven't got time to attend to the IT aspects myself these days, the businesses have become too demanding. And as I said, I'm not impressed by the people who do it now.'

Shane, who had remained silent and seemed to have decided to sit back and listen, just nodded, so after a few more minutes of asking questions and making notes, Arapera got to her feet and reached out to shake Ms Carlson's hand. 'I noticed that your notes mention the number of changes you estimate will happen each month, so we'll read it properly and get in touch with a proposal.'

They assured each other that it had been a pleasure to meet, that they looked forward to seeing each other again to discuss the next step and then Ms Carlson left, inscrutable and immaculate in her cropped, tailored jacket and pencil skirt, and of course, matching high heels. Shades of Jackie Kennedy, thought Arapera, very elegant, and I'd love to find out where she got the suit.

Chapter 8

After the heated, verging on out of control and very loud confrontation with Shane after Ms Carlson's departure, Arapera returned to her little team with a feeling of disbelief. Sinking down on her chair she leaned forward and for a moment considered putting her head down on her keyboard and trying to have a nap. The held-back emotion, the effort to remain calm and reasonable and the strength it took to not rise to Shane's furious accusations made her feel exhausted on top of a sleepless night.

'Here,' said a voice at her side. 'Cheer up - I made us all coffee and Bugsy ran down and bought almond croissants.'

Thomas put her cup on the desk and moved his own chair closer and Bugsy scooted his across the open space to sit opposite Arapera in the formation they always used when they discussed a problem or worked out how to divide a big project between them.

'OK, tell us what's going on. We heard Shane yelling, so something in that meeting lit the fuse. Was it you or Ms What's-her-name, that woman whose business we still don't know anything about? Bugsy googled her name and found nothing more interesting than the fact that she got a business degree from Vic about fifteen years ago.'

'Smashing legs,' said Bugsy dreamily. 'What a classy lady! But what's going on? From the volume of Shane having a go at you, they probably heard him down on the street.'

Arapera sat up straighter and smiled at their curious faces and blessed her luck to have two such nice guys to work with.

'I'll tell you practically word for word what was said in the meeting with Ms Carlson *and* the aftermath – but on one condition. And I mean this, I'm very serious – you must *never* let on that I told you. If Shane thought I had, it would make him feel even more undermined that he does now – and he does feel seriously threatened. He accused me of hijacking the meeting and putting him on the back foot and being devious. All of which I freely admit. I was hoping to make it impossible for him not to ask for that software we want, so I behaved pretty badly, but it would be worth it if we get what we need. Because I have a feeling that Ms Carlson could become a valuable client – and she's very smart, and I think there's more to those unidentified businesses than she let on. And she'd make sure we had what I indicated we had, or would get, in the way of software now that she's heard my sales pitch for it. If someone with five business entities, soon to become seven, made it a condition to hire us then my plan might work.'

But however calmly she told the story of how the meeting had given her such a perfect opportunity to out-manoeuvre Shane, she knew she had probably risked too much, and it might end badly for her personally. Given Shane's tendency to dither about decisions, combined with how furious he was now, it might develop into a complaints issue, just so he could hand it over to someone else to deal with, which meant either the **HR** manager or the **CEO**.

The email that she had hoped would not arrive, pinged into her Inbox at lunch time; the CEO requested that she meet with him at three that afternoon and that she "be prepared to explain her behaviour in a recent meeting with a potential new client".

'Guys – listen. Do me a favour and make sure you're very industrious for the rest of today, heads down, hands on your mouse, no chatter - and be polite if Shane pops his head around the door. I've got to justify my behaviour to the CEO at three, and I need to prepare what I'll say.'

She waved away their questions and told them to

leave her to think, tilted her chair back and rested her left foot on the pulled out bottom drawer in her desk while she considered her options. There had been no indication if the meeting would be with Blair Strom alone or if it would include Shane or the HR manager, and she needed two ways of presenting how she saw things depending on who was in the room at the time. After ten minutes of letting those scenarios play out in her mind, she decided to go one step further than either Shane or the CEO might expect. She spent half an hour composing a document where she outlined the rationale for buying the new software and what the benefits would be, followed by a display of the comparative costs of buying it outright and pay for support or leasing it at a monthly fee and getting the support free. This she followed up with a summary of her earlier discussions with Shane, carefully worded, strategically lowkey and non-judgemental. After reading it twice she heaved a sigh of relief; it was a fair summary of what had preceded the Carlson meeting. She emailed it as an attachment to the CEO with a blind copy to her own private email address and printed a copy, just in case.

Picking the paper off the printer, she slid her phone into her pocket and smiled at Thomas who was watching her with a worried frown. 'Thank goodness you guys gave me morning tea – I forgot to have lunch today. I'll show you what I've written up when I get back.'

On the way upstairs, her phone signalled a message from Carmen asking if she wanted to meet for an early meal at Apache, and she fired off a 'yes please' to her and an 'out for dinner' message to Carter, pleased at the prospect of some light relief at the end of the day.

I'm glad I was prepared, thought Arapera when she entered the CEO's office. The expression on Blair Strom's face was openly hostile and he started talking without greeting her, his voice so aggressive and brusque that Arapera's heart sank.

'I've had a serious complaint from Shane about your appalling behaviour in a meeting with a prospective client this morning – and other things.'

He leaned forward over his desk and stabbed his forefinger into the sheet of paper in front of him. 'Shane has provided a formal complaint form with all the details of what went on when you two met with Ms Carlson, and all I can say is that your behaviour is completely unacceptable. You undermined your manager in front of a client, which amounts to unprofessional conduct. You have also – over a period of time – exerted ongoing pressure on Shane, both in person and via your team, to spend a considerable sum on new software, which he assures me we don't need. What have you got to say?'

He's made his mind up, thought Arapera, he's going to give me a warning or fire me - and I doubt there's anything I can do about it. But I'll damn well have a good try.

'I sent you a document earlier that gives the background of how I see it,' she said and tried to keep her voice calm and reasonable. 'I admit I have overstepped the line, but I feel the provocation has been severe. All my well informed and well-based suggestions about updating to new software have been met with nothing but evasions - and no serious consideration has been given to verbal or written requests for an in-depth discussion about it.'

'Stop right there! Shane assures me he's considered your suggestions seriously, given you adequate reasons why he feels the expense is totally unnecessary – and then, even after that, you side-line him in a client meeting and make him look ridiculous! I'm giving you a formal warning and you'll be having performance reviews three-monthly.'

'Would you please read the document I sent you?' she asked with a sinking heart and a feeling of doom. 'Be fair - at least read my side of it before you make a decision.'

Blair raised his pompous bulk and stood behind his desk like a judge about the dismiss the court before leaving the courtroom. 'I have said all I have to say, Arapera. You can go back to your work.'

Shane was very good at making himself look ridiculous without any help from her, thought Arapera going down in the lift, it was a natural talent, and she should have known better than think that Blair would read her rationale before acting in such a draconian manner. God knows what it was about Shane that made him so precious to the upper echelons. She had sometimes wondered if he was the nephew or brother-in-law of someone important in the company, though Theresa claimed he was not.

I must stop doing half his job for him, thought Arapera vengefully, and let him try to get things done himself and then we'll see how long it is before he panics. Useless little man!

'Don't get your hopes up,' she said when she got back to her desk and met the questioning looks from two pairs of eyes. 'I've been given a first warning and I'm on performance reviews every three months.'

'For fuck's sake! That prick!' Thomas leapt to his feet and looked as if he was about to punch someone. 'You're a top asset and they treat you like that? I can't believe it! And just to protect that little twit we're supposed to call a manager.'

'Calm down, please, not so loud,' said Arapera quietly. 'If Shane hears you, you'll be in trouble too, and I'll be charged with conspiracy and rabble rousing or some damn thing. I've admitted I went too far, and I would apologise if I thought it would help. But now I'm going to put my head down and work for the rest of the afternoon, and then I'll go home and think about my options.'

She put down the paper she hadn't even remembered she had in her hand, when she stood in front of Blair, and turned to her screen.

Chapter 9

A rriving slightly late at Apache for dinner with
Carmen, Arapera couldn't see her and sent a
text asking if she had reserved a table or if she should
go in and get one. The reply was instant, "Already here,
far back, waving."

Arapera walked down to the length of the long
room towards the arm that waved above a mass of
shocking pink hair, shaking her head.

'You've done it again!' she exclaimed when she
reached Carmen's table. 'I should have asked what
colour your hair is when we made the date. Last time
you had bright blue hair and I didn't recognize you,
now it's furious pink – for God's sake, Carmen, if you
keep this up your hair will fall out.'

Carmen jumped to her feet and hugged Arapera
hard. 'God, I'm so glad you're all right! I couldn't

believe those videos – you must have been so scared under that car.'

'Videos? Are there videos?'

Carmen's partner Ollie, who hardly ever said anything, just ate a lot and occasionally put his phone down, looked up from the screen and grinned. 'Of course, there are videos. Does anything happen that doesn't end up in a video on social media? Awesome scene – like something out of a film – I wish I'd been there. Bet you were terrified.'

'But I haven't seen any videos,' said Arapera with a feeling of vague unease. 'When did they pop up? And where?'

Carmen shrugged. 'Oh, sometime today, I think. I only heard about them when Ollie sent me a link from work at lunchtime – everyone's talking about them. There have been so many shares on Facebook and Twitter it's probably everywhere now – and it's on YouTube too and Insta. I keep going back and looking at them because it's so unbelievable that you didn't get crushed. It's truly like a miracle, just as they say – someone was looking after you.'

It wasn't until they were halfway through the meal that Arapera thought of the obvious. 'Ollie, can you show me one of those videos? I'd love to have a look right away, so I can check on those two girls. I'd like to see for myself that they're safe.'

'Of course,' Ollie picked up his phone from the

table and Carmen looked hard at Arapera. 'What girls?'

'Those girls I tried to shove to one side, you know – one split second before that car nearly hit us.'

The way Carmen was looking at her was not just disconcerting, it made her feel alarmed. 'What? Why are you looking like that?'

'Here it is.' Ollie handed her his phone. She started the video, stopped it after a few seconds, re-started it from the beginning and then a third time. She sat there with her head bent over the phone, unwilling to look up, while confused thoughts swirled in her head. The video started before the car hit the edge of the pavement as if someone had noticed it accelerating across the street at an angle and just lifted their phone and pressed 'record'.

'You knew, didn't you? You figured it out the moment I said, "those girls". Because there were no girls.' Arapera looked into her friend's serious eyes, and they nodded at each other.

'Yeah, I did,' said Carmen. 'I've been trying to figure out what it was you did before you fell, and the car tipped over you. It's been on my mind all afternoon. I told Ollie I couldn't work it out and we watched it several times just before you arrived, well, both the videos – but the second one only shows she scene from the time the front of the car hit that ledge, not the part where you say you saw the girls.' She looked at Ollie, who nodded confirmation and said, 'The way you leap to one side and your left arm swings out and you twist in mid-air – as if you're pushing something invisible away from being hit by the car.'

Then Carmen's expression, which so far had remained concerned and slightly puzzled, switched to excited. 'And you say you saw two girls - so you leapt to save them from being hit by the car?'

It was easy to see that both Carmen and Ollie were fascinated by the idea that Arapera had seen something that wasn't there, but to her it was confusing and slightly scary.

'But I *did* see two girls – I did, I'm not making it up. Both had ponytails, one blondish and one a bit darker, about nine or ten - they *were* there, just beside me!'

Arapera heard her own voice rising and tried to regain her composure, while Carmen, whose belief systems included many non-mainstream components, reached out a tattooed arm and patted Arapera's hand. 'They were ghosts, of course - must've been. I know you don't believe in ghosts, but lots of people do – clever and reasonable people like me, not just crazies. And what else could it be? I bet Dan got a shock when he heard.'

'I'm not with Dan any longer – I broke it off a while ago when he went to the South Island.'

'You didn't! Why? He was such a nice guy – and why didn't you tell me?'

'He wasn't as nice as he seemed, Carmen, far from it! And when I found out what he was really like behind that smooth facade, I told him it was over. Thank God, I'm flatting with Carter and the flat's mine, or I might have moved in with Dan already and it would have got complicated.'

Carmen, who was always able to read Arapera like an open book, studied her face for a moment in silence before she spoke. 'Well, never mind about Dan – I'll take your word for it, but it's sad to lose such a piece of eye candy. But to get back to things that matter, do tell us again how it felt, you know, when you pushed those girls to one side. Did it feel as if you pushed something physical – or did your arm kind of swipe through air as if nothing was there?'

It was hard to know how to answer, because in Arapera's mind there was a gap of a second or two and she had no retained impression of her arm striking anything, or of the car tilting over her.

They were still talking about it an hour later and after two glasses of wine and having been unable to eat more than half her meal, Arapera knew it was time to go home. If I didn't have a sore ankle I'd walk, she thought, it's a lovely evening and it's only about one kilometre from here to the flat, but I'd better get a taxi, I don't feel like waiting for the bus. She regretted not being able to walk home because she found solitary walks helpful for sorting things out in her mind, and she wondered how many miles she had covered since her childhood. Hundreds of kilometres, she thought, no, thousands, and when I think how far I went from home and sometimes quite late, but nobody asked me where I had been - it seems amazing now.

'Please don't talk about it,' she said as they parted outside. 'Comment if it comes up, but *please* don't tell anyone that you know what I saw. I need to get my head around this – I can't explain it and it scares me to even think of what the explanation might be. I'm either having a breakdown or going mad and hallucinating. I mean, seeing things that other people can't see! Too weird - I need time to get used to it.'

Chapter 10

Going to work the next morning was hard, with apprehension about the day ahead at the forefront of her mind. Having dressed in her new charcoal grey jeans and ankle boots to bolster her confidence, she sat on the bus and stared absently at the pedestrians' coats flapping in the blustery wind.

Even just thinking of being reduced to having three-monthly performance reviews made her feel that she couldn't possibly put up with it, it was too humiliating to bear at this stage of her career, so it was probably better to leave even without a new job to go to. The gossip would spread, and though many in the other teams would applaud her daring, they would also pity her, and she doubted if she could cope with that. Criticism or disapproval she could cope with, but pity was one step too far.

. . .

That morning Arapera had desperately wanted to talk to Carter about what had happened, but he hadn't come home until very late, and today he was on the early shift, so she never saw him at all.

Sometimes she asked where he had been after a new date, hoping he would tell her about some interesting man he had met, but he always said the same thing: 'Just sitting quietly reading Jane Austen in the library. You know me – I forgot the time and got locked in when they closed.'

Talking things over with Carter had always been her reality check when something happened at home or if she was worried, but not for a long time had she felt the need to use him as a sounding-board as much as she did now. They had been firm friends since high school when he, two years older, was hesitant about coming out as gay, and she agreed to act as if she were his girlfriend, which included a romantic performance on the dance floor at the senior ball. Their close relationship had lasted over the years, and both had cried on the shoulder of the other when they were sad and upset. There was nobody in the world she would rather talk to just now, and one of his hugs would have made her feel a lot better.

Her little team of two seemed to have agreed to not talk about the events of yesterday, which took a weight off her mind, because at least she could carry on with work and pretend it was just another ordinary day. At morning teatime Bugsy bought her a take-out coffee and a chocolate chip biscuit from the café downstairs, Thomas said how much he liked her new striped shirt, and then they talked about work and how to solve the problem of a supposedly automatic software update, that for some reason hadn't happened.

'Well, we've got the update now,' said Bugsy reasonably. 'I think we should just go back and scan for those two functions the patch was for - in everything we've done since. It's not as if we've had time to produce a lot of new stuff since this was discovered.'

Shane's door was shut and none of them realised he was not in his room until Theresa put a call through to Arapera just before lunch. 'This woman wants to talk to Shane, but he's home sick – can you take it?'

'Good morning, Ms Woodhill. Thank you for taking my call – I just want to ask a couple of questions about our meeting yesterday,' said a voice she instantly recognised a Fiona Carlson's distinctive delivery, quiet and with hardly any emphasis placed any one word.

'Of course, I'm happy to help you if I can, Ms Carlson,' said Arapera and wondered what was coming, hopefully nothing that would necessitate talking about the new software again.

'Who will be directly responsible for the work if I move to your firm? Is it you or Mr McDonald? Or someone else in your team?'

Caught in a classic cleft stick situation, Arapera

hesitated and knew she must be very circumspect now that her job was on the line. 'Mr McDonald is the head of the section, so he would ultimately be responsible.'

'Yes, but who would I deal with about practical issues regarding changes, who would I be talking to on a day-to-day basis?'

Oh shit, thought Arapera desperately, I don't want to lie, and I don't want to say something that gives the game away in front of the boys. I'll have to give her a hint without saying anything definite.

She got up, picked up her empty glass and walked out into the corridor while she spoke. 'I can't actually give you a definitive answer right now. I'm not sure who it will be – normally it would have been me, but I there's a possibility that I might not be here.'

Without sounding surprised Ms Carlson said, 'Could you meet me for lunch? In about an hour? And let's use first names – I'm Fiona.'

A minute later Arapera put the phone on top of the water cooler and filled her glass feeling slightly detached from reality. The short conversation with Fiona had an Alice of Wonderland quality, as surprising as it was entertaining. She couldn't tell the boys who the call was from, or they would prod for answers, and she wanted to find out what this was about before she gave them as much as a hint either that she was contemplating resigning or that she was having lunch with Fiona. She had no clear idea of what was in Fiona's mind, but before she went out, she must do two things.

With the glass in her hand and the phone in her pocket, she continued out to the lobby and said casually to Theresa, 'I must go and sign a couple of things at the bank in my lunch hour, but you know how it is these days. The banks have hardly any staff because we all do everything online, so if I have to wait, I might be a bit late back. And with Shane away today, perhaps put any calls for him through to the top floor? Or to Andrew?'

Theresa winked. 'Sure - we don't want your boys getting above themselves.'

Arapera took a sip of water and tried to sound as if she was idly asking and not really interested, 'Who was it - that call you put through? We got cut off for some reason.'

'I've no idea – if it's important she'll call back,' said Theresa, and Arapera went back to her room, satisfied that whatever this lunch meeting was about, nobody at work would find out that she had talked to Ms Carlson.

Chapter 11

Walking the short distance to the Capital on the Quay mall Arapera wondered if Fiona had noticed her limp and chosen something close on purpose. The pavement was crowded with shoppers and people out in their lunch breaks, taking advantage of the lovely weather. The shop windows were full of summer fashions, and it was tempting to do more than glance at them, but she kept a steady pace close to the walls to avoid faster walkers bumping into her. A stumble now and further injury to her ankle was the last thing she needed. Riding up the escalator at the mall, Arapera speculated about the reason for the invitation, but reached no conclusion, other than the possibility that Shane's behaviour had puzzled Fiona and she wanted reassurance that the company was able to deliver to her requirements. Why this had resulted in an invitation for lunch seemed quite odd, but someone as mysterious as Fiona Carlson, who obviously played her cards close to her chest, was hard to second-guess.

Fiona was waiting outside the café looking immaculate in a pale blue suit instead of yesterday's grey one and with another pair of very expensive looking high heels, Arapera spotted her as soon as her head rose above floor level and thought that she had never known anyone so glamorous and so well dressed; it intrigued her, made her think of high-flying woman lawyers in movies, women who owned private jets. Or maybe, she thought, women whose husbands owned private jets. And so far, she knew nothing about Fiona, she could be a drug dealer or an art dealer, anything was possible. This is like an adventure, thought Arapera and smiled, or a surprise party and anything could happen.

'Hi Arapera,' said Fiona and gestured for Arapera to go ahead of her. 'I'm glad you could come at such short notice. I've booked that table in the far corner over there so we can have some privacy.'

Ten minutes later, after they had ordered food and been given glasses of water, she looked calmly at Arapera across the table and asked without preamble, 'Would you like to come and work for me?'

It took Arapera by surprise, such a sudden question with no lead-in, no explanation and no attempt to find out what Arapera's plans were. It made her laugh and Fiona Carlson smiled and said, 'Well? You're contemplating leaving, aren't you? But I don't know if you have another job to go to or one you hope to get – maybe you have applied for one? But whatever the situation, I want to offer you a job.'

'Why?' asked Arapera, while in the back of her mind she wondered what Fiona's business was and how she could possibly know if she wanted to work with someone about whom she knew nothing. It would be a leap in the dark, but at least she knew that Fiona was smart and likeable. Maybe she could?

'I do understand that you know nothing about me or what I do,' said Fiona calmly. 'I'll tell you what I do, and you can ask anything you like – I want you to feel you can trust me. Put that question about a job on hold, and I'll start again. Yesterday I could read the relationship between you and your manager like an open book, it was written on both your faces – that guy is ineffectual and finds it hard to get his thoughts into enough order to put them into words, *and* he's indecisive – while you are mentally organised and smart and *quick*. You clearly had an agenda about that software you talked about, so I imagine you took the opportunity to push him a bit in front of a client – or potential client. Am I right?'

Arapera nodded. 'Yes, exactly right. So, tell me why you're offering me a job when you said yesterday that you didn't want the IT function in-house.'

'I changed my mind after the meeting – I really enjoyed your tactics and your smart opportunity grab to promote that new software you want. I think you're just the sort of person I could work closely with. I have five businesses, as I said, each one a separate entity and I run them from my house, I have an outside accounting firm to do the financial accounts at year-end and I do the rest myself. I'm a trained accountant, and the only reason I don't the annual financials and the tax and company reporting etc is that I just can't be bothered. Same with the IT work – and that's got much more complex, so I farmed it out. But you could do it as and when it needs doing, and I'd have you there to discuss things with. I don't want my entire life taken over by my business – and working from home makes that a possibility, or a risk. I don't need a fulltime IT person, but you're just the right sort of person who could do other things for me as well, interesting things that we'll talk about later.'

A waiter arrived with their food before Arapera could ask any questions and there was a pause while they unfolded napkins, picket up cutlery and settled down.

'So,' continued Fiona, 'the next thing you'll want to know is what my businesses are. But instead of telling you right now, I'd like to tell the story of how it started. Because it's such a great story and I very rarely, if ever, get a chance to tell it.'

Arapera waited, eating suspended and her gaze riveted on Fiona's face. This was the most unusual meeting she could ever have imagined in the context of job searches or job interviews. Not only was Fiona the most intriguing person she had ever met, but the whole situation made her feel as if she were in a movie or a novel. Who knew what might happen next?

'My great-uncle Jim never married, and he had no children,' said Fiona. 'He lived in a small town in Wairarapa and had a sprawling second-hand shop, like Aladdin's cave – treasure heaped on treasure mixed with a lot of junk. To start with he lived in a house on a side street – this is before I can remember him – and then he bought the building next to his shop in the main street and linked them with a wide passage – which later turned out to be illegal because he built it himself without consent from the county, but never mind. The second property was two-storied, so he lived upstairs, expanded the business into the second house and sold his house on the side street. Over the years he built an extension out the back of the original shop when he needed even more room to store and display things. He bought house lots when people cleared out old relatives' houses and he was very popular with the ever-increasing number of people from Wellington, who go to the Wairarapa wine-country in the weekends.'

Arapera made no comment while Fiona stopped to take a bite of food, she just quietly ate her corn fritters with salsa and waited for this amazing tale to be continued.

'So,' continued Fiona after a few mouthfuls, 'when I was twenty-six, great-uncle Jim asked me to come and stay at a B&B down the road from his shop and spend a week with him, he said he'd pay, and it was important that I came. I had no idea why he asked, but I'd always loved the shop, and I quite liked him - and it was an intriguing invitation, so I took a week's leave and did what he asked.'

She drank some water, took another bite and carried on. 'Jim said he was leaving me the business and the buildings in his will. His other young relations had no real connection – they'd never visited him, he didn't know them, but he felt that he'd seen enough of me over the years to see that I was interested in old things when my parents took me to see him, or we called in on our way to Hawke's Bay. And from then until he died, I went up there for a weekend nearly every month and he taught me a lot.'

'You were the relative he chose to carry on. What a lovely story,' said Arapera, but Fiona wasn't finished. 'He died two years later, just months after my grandfather, who was his only brother, and I inherited the lot – the business, two properties, an illegal connecting passage, and the contents of his upstairs flat, which I will tell you about later, but let's just say that was the *real* Aladdin's cave. And for a couple of years, I tried to live there and run it, but it was never going to work – I'm too fond of living in Wellington, I like being in a city, not a small town, and I didn't want to run a shop - and I missed my friends and the restaurants. But those two years were usefully spent learning more about old things, antique or not – about crystal and silver and porcelain. I learnt what is desirable and where in the world the buyers are, how to get valuations done and how to research the provenance of an object and get it documented.'

She took another bite and smiled. 'I had no idea how much I didn't know. It was an enormous learning curve, like being back at school, and the more I learnt, the more I found I must study further – and I'm still doing it. And of course, I sorted and categorized things, got rid of truckloads of rubbish while I tried to figure out how to run the business without a physical shop – selling precious objects online is very different from selling shoes.'

She grinned across the table and Arapera suddenly saw a completely new Fiona, transformed by remembered excitement and joy with no trace of her usual calm and controlled expression. 'I told you it was a long story, didn't I? And it's not finished yet, that was just the beginning, setting the scene so you understand how I got into this.'

She raised her hand above her head and within what seemed like seconds a waiter came over, and Arapera thought, I bet that happens wherever she is – she lifts a finger and they come hurrying towards her. Fiona leaned towards Arapera and said, as if she was sharing a closely guarded secret, 'I'm going to do something I only do once or twice a year, at times when

I'm celebrating something, and I think today might turn out to be one of those days.'

Turning to the waiter she said, 'Can we have two of those special doughnut buns – I can't remember what they're called – and two table knives please. And coffee – Arapera, how do you take yours?'

As soon as the waiter left, Fiona made a face and exclaimed, 'Oh my God, you're not on a diet, are you? I should have asked! Because there's no way I can eat two of those things. They are delicious – like a big doughnut without the hole and cut in half with raspberry jam and masses of fresh whipped cream inside. I don't know how they do it, but they're different from everywhere else, much lighter and much less oily. And don't worry, they're probably only a thousand calories, most of it sugar and fat, so nothing to worry about.'

Arapera smiled at this unexpected side of the perfect Ms Carlson. 'I love doughnuts, too and ...' But before she could continue Fiona's phone buzzed and she glanced at it, then at Arapera. 'Sorry, but I've got to take this.'

She walked away talking in a low voice to someone, who spoke so loudly that Arapera could hear the voice, if not the words.

Chapter 12

F iona returned a few minutes later, sat down and put the phone in her bag. 'Apologies, I don't like doing that, but sometimes you have to. I didn't mute it because I've been chasing that guy for nearly a week and he's never available. He placed the winning bid on my car on TradeMe, and I want to get things sorted before I go to Australia, but we've had trouble getting coordinated. Now, where had I got to?'

'You inherited the business and sorted things,' said Arapera and Fiona nodded. 'That's it – so, now I live in a house in Wadestown, which I bought mostly because it was a small house on a big section with enough flat ground to build a storage facility behind the house. Yes, I know it sounds mad, but what I've got now is a super safe place with six rooms to store valuable things - with all the bells and whistles like sprinklers in case of fire, CCTV, alarm system set up in sections, linked to my phone and my computer. And each room in the shed, as I call it, contains the stock of one business – at the moment …'

The waiter was back and Arapera studied the creation on the plate he put in front of her and said, 'You're clearly a world authority on doughnuts – this looks amazing.'

'It's like eating clouds with filling – you eat yours and I'll have mine at intervals, so I can continue talking. I recommend slicing it up before you start, or you'll end up with cream and icing sugar all over your face. Anyway, now I have five businesses – silver, crystal and porcelain, rare books, jewellery and signs. I'm hoping to add Art Deco and pottery soon - and I'm vaguely thinking of old New Zealand maps.'

'But how does it work? I presume each business sells and maybe buys online? And you dispatch things from your shed as you call it?'

'I do.' Fiona wiped icing sugar from her fingers and drank some of her coffee. 'And I also dress in track pants and a sweatshirt and fossick though second-hand shops and op-shops all over the place – you know, so I don't look as if I'm a serious collector or something. Twice a year I go to Australia and visit lots of small towns, which is where I find the real old treasures that nobody realises are valuable - I've found some amazing things there. Now I have fantastic websites, one for each business, with images and provenance written up, photos of actual valuations by specialists etc. It's all there. No prices displayed, though – if you're a buyer you can make an offer, and if I like what they offer, I sell the item to them.'

'Yesterday you said something like "if I wanted to offer a second one at half price" – so that was just a ruse, wasn't it? Just to have some kind of example of what we might need to update?'

'Oh yes, most of what I gave as examples was just rubbish. I never reveal what I do until I'm sure that I can trust people to keep their mouths shut. That would have been step two in the discussion I started with your company - if we had continued, which now seems unlikely. The value of my stock and where I live is a secret I keep well under wraps. What I really need is someone who can take over building new websites and updating things, load photos, keep all online functions secure and lots more. Just entering meta data and key words can take ages. The phone apps are invaluable to me, I track all the background data and people use them a lot – maybe to show each other things they've seen on the website, or to show their husband what they bought before it arrives or whatever. But very high traffic. So even if something's been bought, the photo stays up – but no mention of what it sold for, just "sold" and a date. I don't want people to look back at how much something went for earlier. So, your job would involve the analytical side as well.'

'My God, it's the most wonderful story I ever heard! I'd love to work for you. I got such a bollocking from the CEO after my manager complained about my behaviour – you can't imagine. I knew I was inviting trouble in that meeting, and I took the risk knowingly, but now I'm suddenly on three-monthly performance reviews and they've giving me a written first warning - well I haven't had it in writing yet, but it's probably on my desk as we speak.'

'OK, great! When can you start?'

Arapera pretended to think for a moment. 'Tomorrow?' And they both laughed.

'I'm going a scouting trip to Australia in a couple of weeks, and an old friend is minding the business for me, she comes to live in my house when I go away. But I'll be in touch as soon as I get back. Are you going to be OK for money until then – I mean, if you lose your job? It might be a few weeks before I'm able to have you come and work with me. I want to show you everything myself – not that Andrene isn't fully au fait with the business, but you're also going to do the IT stuff, which she doesn't do. As things are now, when Andrene is looking after the place and shipping things out to buyers, I sit in my motel room at night updating the websites and trying to do what needs doing. Which I wouldn't have to do if you were there. But I got side-tracked – are you going to be OK for money if you resign before I get back?'

'Oh, I think so, but I might have to work it out in detail. It depends on if my boss withholds my accumulated holiday pay, which sits at about four weeks right now. He has the right to do that if I resign without giving notice, it's in my contract - and he's a vengeful man, so it's probably a given.'

She paused for a moment before she changed the topic. 'And now, I'd like to ask you something,' she said, finally prepared to voice what she had wondered about since Fiona described her business in detail. 'Because what you've told me doesn't add up. You can't possibly send out so many parcels each day that it amounts to fulltime work – or add so many objects to your websites and database that you need someone to help with it.'

She studied Fiona's face that now had the expression of calm control she had displayed in the meeting with Shane, impossible to read. 'And the rest of the IT work wouldn't take enough time to be a fulltime job – nowhere near it. So, however much you like going to town and meeting friends – it just doesn't add up. So why do you need me?'

Fiona started to laugh and once again changed in a moment from displaying a façade to being a woman thoroughly enjoying herself. 'I wondered how long it would be before you started wondering about that – and what fantastic ideas you might come up with to account for the discrepancies! But rest assured, I'm not a secret assassin for hire or a hooker, I'm a forensic accountant as well.'

Now Arapera was laughing too. 'You're what? Is there really such a thing as a forensic accountant?'

'Oh yes, it's a real thing and I've been doing it for

years. Not with one of those big firms that specialise, just as a sole practitioner. I did auditing, before I left historical accounting — what you'd probably call "regular accounting" — so I was already interested in fossicking around in people's financial lives. And now I spend at least half my time working as a contractor or a consultant, sometimes more.'

'But what do you do? Do you work with the police?'

'I take a variety of jobs when offered, if it suits my schedule of other jobs, and I charge pretty high, because it turns out I'm good at it and quick. Sometimes criminal stuff, like fraud or scams. Sometimes it's a scammer who says he lost all his ill-gotten gains, sometimes it's a family dispute or money gone missing from a deceased's estate. Now and then it's a bankruptcy where the losses don't add up and someone has stashed away a little fortune. And I'll correct myself, it's not only males of course, increasing numbers of con artists are women — they con relatives, or steal huge sums from their employers who totally trust them to run the admin functions, or they pretend to be investment advisors — endless options for dishonest people to get rich. And *that's* why I need you.'

'I *was* getting concerned,' said Arapera. 'Not that I thought you were a freelance assassin but more because you might offer me fulltime employment out of pity or something — which I couldn't agree to.'

Fiona looked at her with something like pride. 'I *knew* I was right about you! I sat in that boring meeting and thought that you're probably exactly what I need – which I know now for a fact. I'll give you my mobile number and we'll arrange for you to come to my place, so I can show you how it works before I go away, if you're interested in an advance tour. We can discuss your pay situation then.'

Fiona got to her feet. 'And I've just realised I didn't tell you the best bit about Jim's flat upstairs. It was literally crammed with silver and crystal and all kinds of valuable stuff that he'd come across over the years and kept aside - things he thought would become even more valuable over time. He just made a decision that those things were his and not the property of the business and moved them upstairs! I've got some photos I took of his flat before I started sorting it out. I'll show you when you come over.'

'I like Jim more every minute,' said Arapera and grinned. 'What a cool great-uncle he was!'

They exchanged phone numbers and parted outside the mall, leaving Arapera feeling as if she had won the lottery.

Chapter 13

Soldierpilotpilot **(289330 followers)**
#coolchick
#thequeenofcool

There is a lot of discussion going on right now on all social media about the phenomenon referred to as "deep fake", after the recent revelation that a press release supposedly from 10 Downing Street, which included a video of some museum opening after renovations, was faked. The British Prime Minister wasn't present, he was two hundred miles away, and the guy who cut the ribbon was the local Member of Parliament. A deep-faker, or whatever we should call these people, swopped his head for that of the Prime Minister so successfully that you can't even tell. And not only that, but they also synched the Prime Minister's mouth movements to match the genuine opening speech. Then they inserted a very scantily clad model to replace the wife of the guy who actually did declare the museum re-opened, and the result was confusion, embarrassment and a rumour storm of no mean proportions.

Clear as mud? Good!

So, here's a challenge for all the nerds in the world, those who aren't working away at their desks creating deep fake videos and causing chaotic situations for politicians and film stars. Could you please design some little software gizmo or app or whatever the hell you want to call it, something us ordinary punters can download and use to check if stuff is genuine or if it's been tampered with. If you can't, I think I can guarantee that making decisions about your vote in the next election might as well be done by your five-year old or by looking for omens in the sky and studying the entrails of grey geese.

Back to more about the Queen of Cool next time, I just had to get this of my chest before I choked on it.

And a PS to an earlier blog: some claimed they were baffled by my mention of a clever Twitter handle. Here's the solution: don't pronounce it cosmo-zero, say cosmo-nought — it was a nice way of using the slashed zero.

Chapter 14

When Arapera stopped in the half-open door to Blair's office and knocked before walking in, Blair's expression instantly switched from his normal pompous look to impatient, and he nearly shouted, 'I am *not* arguing about this, Arapera! The issue is *closed*, and I will not debate it again!'

Arapera, giving him a little smile that she hoped looked calm and faintly amused, said quietly, 'I'm not here to do any debating - I'm doing you the courtesy of telling you in person that I'm resigning as of the end of this afternoon. You will have it in writing before five.'

His expression turned thunderous, and colour rose in a red tide from his shirt collar up his neck to his face. 'I hope you realise that if you resign without giving due notice, I have the right to withhold your holiday pay.' His voice was vicious, and she could just about hear the unspoken last sentence, 'And let's see how you like that!'

'Of course,' she said, openly amused now that he had betrayed his bad temper and his rudeness while she had remained calm and managed to keep her voice even. 'I wouldn't expect anything less.' She left the unspoken words, 'from you' floating in the air between them and walked out.

As soon as she got back to her desk, she wrote and printed her resignation letter and showed it to Thomas and Bugsy. Defusing their anger took more than a few minutes and resulted in an impromptu farewell party with the boys and Theresa, after Bugsy went downstairs to the café and returned with a take-out tray of four coffees and a bag of chocolate brownies. Theresa, hearing the details of why Arapera had resigned, suggested that she should send the summary of events leading up to the complaint from Shane to the other section heads. After a discussion with Thomas and Bugsy when Theresa went back out to reception, she sent the email, signed her resignation letter and asked Thomas to deliver it. Then she put her few personal possessions in her shoulder bag, hugged everyone and left. Admittedly it wasn't yet five o'clock, but what could Blair do about it?

Chapter 15

The Soldierpilotpilot blog (328478 followers)

#coolchick

#thequeenofcool

Well, folks – this is interesting and more than slightly odd. A bit like a book my young cousin was telling me about that she's reading on her Kindle. Because now a kind of time-slip theory is emerging after those video clips got posted on social media showing the accident – it looks as if the Queen of Cool saw some girls who had been there, whether an hour earlier or a year earlier, in that exact spot.

Because there were definitely no little girls at risk of being hit by that car, but in the video, we see the Queen of Cool throwing herself (very athletically) diagonally across to the left from her line of progress at the same moment that the car hits the edge of the pavement and starts to tilt towards her. Her left arm swings out in a wide, deliberate arc as if she is pushing something away from herself and from the car. And as the car tips over on its side just half a meter in front of her, she falls on her back toward the tilting car and the front of the car lands on the ledge and rests there, now fully on its side. Then the car settles slightly, which accounts for her foot getting trapped. (link to YouTube below) and she is stuck in the very low wedge-shaped space under the car.

I'm intrigued, and I do agree with those who are fired up with speculation about this, it does look as if she saw something that wasn't there. As I mentioned in the original Queen of Cool post, one of the first things she said to me was, "Oh no, those girls! What happened to the girls? Are they OK?"

And BTW the book my young cousin (she turned 16 last month) was reading is called "The Girl Who Lived Twice" and she so loved the idea that you might wake up one morning and find that time had rewound by exactly a year, or you had slipped into another time stream, a year behind the one you were in to start with, that she zoomed me and told me nearly the whole story. Yes, really - she loves telling me the plot of entire films too, which is how I got to know so much about romantic comedies.

And if you knew all that would happen for a year ahead, how would you use the advance knowledge? Revenge, financial gain, crime? Endless possibilities for an enterprising young woman.

Chapter 15

As soon as Arapera walked into the flat, she knew Carter was excited, because from the age of fifteen he had never been able to hide it when he had something to share.

'What's going on? Have you fallen in love?'

'No, no – but I found something I want to show you. Let's sit down together and check it out on the internet.'

He refused to say more, so Arapera changed into comfortable clothes and padded barefoot back into the living room with her laptop in her hand. 'OK, let's do it now so we can get back to normal – your excitement is like an electric forcefield, I can't wait a moment longer.'

They sat side by side on the sofa and Carter opened a website on his own laptop and pointed. 'This is very, very intriguing – I've read everything relevant to your accident several times and every time it gets better. This blogger's a real star. On social media I can see the comments, but there aren't any on the website, I don't know why.'

He pushed his laptop towards her and got up. 'Start reading where I've left it and read to the last blog he wrote, and I'll get you a glass of wine. The posts that have that "coolchick" hashtag are about you – of course. I saw the videos from the accident on social media and followed some comments people put on Twitter and that led me to this blogger's website.'

Silently Arapera read the blog entries from the first one about the accident to the last one that was written after the videos surfaced. Obviously, the blogger was Liam, who kept her company until they got her out from under the car, and reading his side of the story was fascinating, so restrained and clear, and for her it was like a personal message. She could nearly hear that dark voice and see his face looking in at her sideways, and she realised they had a bond, a connection that linked them, which others who read his blog would not feel. He and she had lived through an hour of danger together, both of them aware that the front of the car might slip off the ledge and crush her if those inside it moved too much, but they had kept up the appearance of calm. That's why I feel I'm linked to him, she thought, we both had that instinctive thing going, that we could cope if we didn't show each other how scary it was. It feels as if we combined our inner resources to conquer fear - and we won.

'So, the guy who was there started blogging about it? Why would he do that?' She kept things deliberately vague with no reference to what she was feeling. The time to go into detail about this might never come, but right then it felt as if her knowledge of that bond was like a talisman, something very private that would keep her safe.

'He seems to be a well-known blogger – and as he points out, normally he writes about other things like the environment, politics and a bit of history, very entertaining and informative – I've been reading bits here and there since I found his website. If you scroll down, you find hundreds of blog posts – probably three years' worth. And he's on all social media, or nearly all, and he gets comments and then discussions start up and they go on and on. Amazing, really. But I've no idea what he is, like what he does for a job. There's very little about his own life. The hashtag is interesting, though. I mean, who calls themselves soldierpilotpilot unless those are jobs they've had – or have?'

'If you want to read comments on the blog site you just click on the little arrow at the bottom right of his blog posts and the comments open up. Thousands of them, endless discussions and debates. This website is very nicely constructed – clever.'

She continued scrolling back, studying dates and

times. 'Hey, did you notice the followers – how many he's got?'

'No, I didn't pay attention to the details – I was too busy reading what he'd written. I only found this about an hour before you got home. I was going to go for a run seeing I'm on the early shift now and come home early, but I got intrigued when I saw that video on Facebook and then it went from there. So, he's got a big audience, has he?'

'Massive now! It's grown by huge increments since this stuff about the accident. So maybe this is what he does for a living – he blogs.'

'But he's got to do something real to earn a living, doesn't he? Like a regular job?'

'If his audience is big and his blogs are frequent, he would know how many people read each blog instalment, or share it, and then he can charge businesses to have ads on his website or to pop up on the righthand side when you go to his page on social media – that's how those ads get there and how you make money if you're successful. You know, companies that sell things that would appeal to his kind of audience would analyse his following, the Google stats etc and do a deal to have their ads on his page. And I bet the fact that there are videos of the accident is what escalated the number who follow him.'

'The things I don't know.' Carter shook his head in pretend dismay. 'You could fill a library not just one book. Do you think we can find out who he is? I mean, like his name.'

'We might, but it doesn't matter. He's probably good at keeping himself anonymous. Now - I've got a whole lot of stuff to tell you. Why don't you go for your run and then we'll make dinner early when you get back?'

Chapter 16

C arter, back from his run, showered and changed in record time. 'Let's make dinner now – I've got such a story to tell. Showing you the blog was just the beginning – the real excitement starts now.'

Arapera looked up from the sofa where she had been sitting trying to find Fiona's websites by googling key words. So far, her success rate was one out of five, she had found the silver business which was called 'Oxford Street Silver' and for some reason she was certain it was one of Fiona's but trying other famous London streets had brought up nothing.

'Oh, I didn't realise there was more excitement to come. It's a bit early, but you've got a story to tell, and I want to celebrate my news with a leisurely dinner and a glass of really good wine. What do you think?'

'Seeing I live with the newly crowned Queen of Cool, I'll make dinner and tell you my news while I cook, and then you can tell me yours while we eat – because for the first time ever I'm going to tell you exactly what happened on my date.'

'Really?' Arapera looked up with a frown. 'Should I be worried? It's got to be either very bad or very good – you've never told me anything before.'

There was no reply, so she remained where she was on the sofa, deep in thought, while he bustled about in at the kitchen end of the room. When he said, 'Well, come here and sit at the table so I can talk to you,' she was miles away in her mind, once again wondering if she had really seen those girls or if she had hallucinated; worried and intrigued in equal measure.

'Right!' said Carter, speaking over his shoulder while he started slicing something with the very large knife he always used, however small the object to be sliced. 'I arranged to meet this guy at a new place in Cuba Street – bar and bistro - so if it turned out good, we could have a meal after the initial drink. I'd been chatting to him quite a bit online – he seemed really nice, about forty-five, a smart and straight-forward kind of person. His profile said he was a dentist, and I liked the look of him. You might not have noticed, but I never go for the pretty boys– I'm drawn to mature guys, and more like myself, honest and plain.'

'Masculine,' said Arapera, and got up to set the table and find the bottle of red wine she had saved for a special occasion. 'That's what you are. Very masculine, which is why you leave so many disappointed women in your wake, sometimes for me to comfort as they emote about you – and all of them use that awful phrase "what a waste" which of course makes me laugh. Seeing this is turning into a special evening, we'll eat at the table instead of on the sofa. Want a glass of wine now?'

'No thanks – if it's one of your special occasion wines I'll wait until we eat.' Carter bent down to get the wok from the cupboard under the sink and his voice disappeared for a second. '…this guy was what he seemed, nice and ordinary, and good company. And a reader! Yay! You wouldn't believe the number of guys I meet who never read – amazing. Anyway, we had a couple of drinks at the bar and decided to have a meal, so we moved to the dining part of the place and discovered, when I said I'd have vegetarian lasagne, that it's his favourite dish too. And so it went on, and we found more and more things we had in common and then I asked where his dentistry clinic, or whatever you call it, is. And he said he'd sold it about six months ago – he used to be upstairs in Willis Street, but now he's a bitcoin broker.'

'I didn't know there was such a thing.' Arapera moved magazines and a laptop to one side and took the cover off the bowl of salted peanuts that was always on the table and helped herself to a few. 'Not that I've taken an interest in cryptocurrencies apart from being appalled by how those super-sized servers all around the world that process the blockchain transactions use more electric power every day of the year than the whole of Europe.'

Carter swung around with a bag of rice in his hand, and some of it spilled like a cascade of heavy confetti on the floor. 'Oh, shit! But is that right – it uses that much power?'

Arapera got up and fetched the broom and dustpan from the corner beside the fridge. 'Yep – pretty much. The decentralised blockchain process requires huge computing sequences, and the servers get really hot, so they're kept in specially air-conditioned facilities – enormous places just crammed full of hot servers. Admittedly the clever set-ups have turbine that use the heat to produce electricity, but not all do. So it's probably not a very green thing to engage in. But I haven't paid much attention to the actual currency. So, tell me how a bitcoin broker works.'

'Well, I never got to find out how a real bitcoin broker works,' said Carter and turned back to his chopping board. 'If there even is such a thing. The guy wasn't really interested in getting to know me at all – he was just after getting to know my money. It all came out by degrees and I was gradually picking up on little signals I didn't like. First, he told me how much he had made on his own initial investment, and then he spun this lovely tale of how he helped a friend who wasn't computer savvy to invest too, and before he knew it, he was "a broker" with lots of clients, managing their investments. And he offered to invest money for me too.

He said he takes a ten per cent commission on their gains.'

'Do you think it's a scam? Is he swindling people?'

'Ha!' said Carter darkly. 'Is he swindling people? Shit, yeah! We ended up with the most embarrassing scene I have ever been part of in a public place – imagine how mortifying if someone I know had been there and seen it! People were taking photos of it, a real brawl – I bet it's all over social media now. Because a guy called Charlie came in, spotted my date and launched into a verbal attack about how he'd been ripped off to the tune of sixteen thousand dollar - at the top of his voice. And then he launched a physical attack as well, which tipped our table over and sent plates flying – a fucking disaster. If I hadn't kind of been part of it – and no, I did no fighting – I would have enjoyed watching the whole thing. I removed myself to one side very fast when I realised what Charlie was about to do. The bitcoin broker wasn't so lucky.'

His head disappeared into the fridge and again his muted voice just reached her. 'I turned in the door as I left and took a photo of the resulting mess, with those guys wrestling on the floor and getting covered in vegetable lasagne. I'll show you in a minute. And, of course, I left him with the bill. And then I called a mate, and we went for pizza and another couple of drinks to compensate.'

Arapera laughed at the mental image of lasagne

carnage and made up her mind to find videos of this spectacular event on the Internet.

'Did you manage to work out what he had done to that other guy?'

Carter was back at the stove stirring and tossing things in the wok and a delicious smell was spreading through the room. 'I think he'd made more from investing Charlie's money than he told him, and he'd kept quite a chunk for himself on top of his so-called commission – not that the details were very clear but definitely fraud.'

'I think it's basically a pyramid scheme, so if more and more people don't invest at the bottom, the value of the bitcoin won't increase. Don't quote me, but I think that's right.'

'Oh, well – the pyramid came toppling down on that scumbag's head last night. I think I'll have to warn my social media friends about him – if I can find something from last night online, I'll share it and I've got that photo of the pasta wrestling, which will make people take notice.'

'This is the best stir-fry you've ever made – delicious!' Arapera put her chopsticks down after a couple of mouthfuls and raised her glass at Carter. 'Different from other times, so you must have added something extra. I'm so lucky you're such a great cook.'

'I don't usually put in both lemon grass and root ginger – that might be it. I'm glad you like it. Now tell me about your exciting day – did it involve promotion and more money?'

'No, the absolute opposite.' She slanted a wry glance at him. 'So opposite it's nearly comical. The story started yesterday with a meeting Shane and I had with a potential new client.'

She related the story chronologically, from the argument with Shane after the meeting to how it culminated with a formal warning and a threat of three-monthly performance reviews.

'It sounds like a serious over-reaction,' said Carter decisively. 'Performance reviews? I mean, what's insubordination got to do with performance? Nothing! That guy was out to penalise you, wasn't he? But why?'

'I used to wonder if Shane has some kind of hold over him. I know I overstepped the mark yesterday, I freely admit it, but there have been other times when he's defended Shane's crazy decisions to the point of being unreasonable. I thought at one time they might be related, but no, they're not – Theresa in reception knows everything, and she said there's no connection.'

'Shane's probably the son of his mistress and that's why nobody knows.' Carter grinned. 'These things happen, you know. But I must admit I'm a bit puzzled by how cheerful you are about this disaster – is there more to come?'

'God yes, a lot more. I didn't see you last night or this morning, and I was dying to discuss if I should resign or not, even before I tried to find another job. I was so over that pompous man! But the woman we had the meeting with called this morning and took me out for lunch.'

The story took a long time to tell and necessitated another glass each of the fabulous red, and by the time Arapera got the resignation scene, they were both laughing.

'What a drama! From total disaster one day to stunning prospects the next – and I can't wait to hear about Fiona's place and what it's like. It sounds like something out of a TV series. A gorgeous lady, *and* kind and clever, living alone with a super secure storage place in her back garden. I wonder what her neighbours think it is. It couldn't be more exciting, could it? And I suppose you'll just resign if it turns out she's really the queen of the capital's drug world?'

They toasted Arapera's future and then Carter turned serious and said, 'Now, let's get back to the incident with "the girls who weren't there" as they call it on social media. I could tell how worried you are about it – it was written all over your face when you read that guy's blog. Please promise you'll tell me if it gets too much. I mean if you need to talk about it or something.'

'Oh, I will – but I'm OK so far.'

She knew she wasn't but talking about it again might ruin this lovely evening, so she got up to take their plates to the kitchen and smiled as she did it.

'Feel like Halo?' asked Carter while she was rinsing their plates. 'We haven't played for ages, and I want to get a bit more experience with choosing the right type of grenade – I think I don't react fast enough to get it right, I just grab one and hope for the best and then it isn't as effective as I hoped it would be.'

'OK, I don't mind, but not another multi-hour session and not getting to bed until two in the morning.

You're starting early tomorrow, remember? And you were out late last night too.'

'Jesus, girl, are you're getting to be just like my mum. Come over here and get your gear out.'

The sat on the sofa side by side with their new Playstation 5 consoles and as usual they got so immersed in Halo that it was half past midnight before they stopped.

'I *love* the gravity hammer,' said Carter and turned the TV off, and just before Arapera disappeared into her bedroom he added, 'And please let me know if you need to talk – I don't want you to suffer in silence. It's not being a wuss, it's more like saying "give me a hug" and you do that all the time without feeling embarrassed.'

'Thanks, and please don't worry – of course, I will.' She smiled and closed the bedroom door behind her, hoping she would be able to sleep, because inside her head the worry about what it was she had seen never ceased, it was like continuous background noise now, always there, sometimes very quiet, sometimes loud and she didn't know how to stop it.

Chapter 18

When Fiona opened the door, Arapera tried to hide a smile; gone was the stylish and immaculate apparition she had met in town, and in front of her stood a barefoot woman with a ponytail, dressed in leggings and a sweatshirt.

Fiona must have caught the amused look because she laughed. 'Welcome to my reality! This is my working garb, usually the only people I see are the couriers who come to pick up parcels – which is why I always dress up when I go to town, it's fun to have a total change - and I love stylish clothes. But come in!'

The interior was a dream of mid-century design. And all genuine, not modern copies, thought Arapera as she looked around. 'Gorgeous!' she said appreciatively. 'The total look. How long did it take you to get it all together?'

'Oh, not long at all. It's mostly from uncle Jim's

shop – I've had some things restored to furnish this house when I bought it. And then I've picked up bits and pieces when I've been traipsing around second-hand shops looking for things for the business. I'm still looking for the perfect bookcase in the right style and size for the guest room.'

They walked down the passage that bisected the house from the front door to the garden at the back, and Fiona opened the door and pointed. 'That's the shed. No point trying to give it a fancy name, it's a very long shed, nearly twenty meters. You can't see the cameras on the corners because they're disguised as part of the guttering, with some clever programming in the movement sensors, so the lights don't react to cats or anything small. I thought if I was going to build it at all, I'd better make it big enough from the start.'

They walked across the damp grass to the door at the short end of the shed, which was at right angles to the house with a tall hedge behind it. 'Sorry about the wet grass.' Fiona keyed in a six-digit pin in the keypad. 'I'm going to put down some pavers. I've got a UPS for the shed because there's so much that relies on power, cameras outside and in, outside lights, electronic locks, air conditioning – and the alarm system, of course. If the power goes out the UPS should keep everything going for a couple of days at least.'

As the door swung open Arapera noticed how thick it was and how it moved, smoothly but like something heavy. 'Reinforced door?'

'Yes, pretty solid and so are the walls – the shed is a bit like a huge freestanding safe.'

In front of them a long corridor ran alongside the right-hand side outer wall with six doors evenly spaced on the left, all with keypads. The light had come on automatically when the door opened, but there were no signs of the windows Arapera had noticed and wondered about from the outside. If the shed was to be totally secure, why have windows?

Fiona gestured at the doors and said, 'Each one uses the same first five digits of the outer door's code and the sixth digit is the number of the specific room. I deliberately have nothing on the doors to identify what's inside. My friend, who comes from Napier to look after the business and lives in the house when I go away, calls me a security freak – and she's right. I try never to leave anything to chance if I can possibly avoid it. But let's go in – we'll start at this end with room number one – signs.'

'So those windows are fake, just for appearance,' said Arapera, 'but why do you have them at all?'

'Oh, just so it looks like a granny flat or something, not too intriguing. And they were easy to mock up. With the venetian blinds half-closed like that you can't tell there's only a wall immediately behind them – the shed looks like a dwelling. That's just in case someone wanders into the back garden looking for mischief – a big shed with no windows would make people wonder what's in it, but now it looks like nothing special.'

The first room had shelves on two walls with signs of various sizes, lined up like books in a bookshelf and a few larger ones leaning against the wall.

'Old signs, rare signs and cult signs, probably about a hundred right now − all of them collectable. The total retail value of this room is only about eighty thousand dollars, this is the least valuable room. But lately I've got a couple of demolition guys acting as agents, I get notified if they come across something really interesting that would normally go to the dump, and they get a finder's fee. They're alpha sorted, so if someone puts in a successful bid on an Edmonds baking powder sign, I know it's stored under the letter E.' She reached out and pulled a tin sign out and held it up for Arapera to see. 'And then you compare the barcode on the back to make sure it's the exact one they bid on.'

'Are all these on the website?'

'No, not at the same time.' Fiona slid the sign back between others in the cubby hole marked E. 'I have several Edmonds signs, slightly different formats and some more damaged, but only one Edmonds at a time on the website. And now for one of the interesting rooms, porcelain and crystal.'

'Oh my God!' Arapera took a step into the second room and turned slowly, trying to take it all in. 'Amazing!'

In a room lined with shelves, objects were lined up

behind glass doors ,with folded bubble wrap between one and the next.

'These doors aren't glass, they're a plastic material, so if things slide in an earthquake, they won't be damaged – and of course the buffers between things are to stop them bumping into each other.' Fiona pointed at the barcodes on the edges of the shelves. 'I just use the barcode reader on my phone to find the right one.'

'Clever!' said Arapera. 'And using those separating cardboard things they put in cartons of wine bottles for the sets of glasses – brilliant idea.'

'I've improved how I do it in the four years since I built the shed,' said Fiona as she unlocked the next room. 'This is my favourite room – the silver room, but everything is kept in cloth bags so they don't tarnish - you'll have to imagine how spectacular it would look with everything exposed. They get couriered in their bags, and carefully packed. And the barcodes are on the shelves here too, so it's easy to locate an item that just sold.'

At the end of an hour Arapera's mind was buzzing with excitement. 'I'm so impressed – it's like a super organized treasure cave,' she said, as she leaned against the kitchen windowsill and watched Fiona making coffee. 'The silver and jewellery rooms – they must be worth a fortune. I presume the neighbours don't know what's in the shed?'

'God, no! Nobody does, only Andrene, she's my friend from Napier, and you and me. I told the people who built the shed that I was going to use it to store seeds for my international seed business - selling seeds from heritage vegetables and native plants. They probably thought I was over cautious.'

She laughed. 'I told them I sell seeds to plant collectors and botanic gardens all over the world and that's why the shed had to be secure and climate controlled. But I only have the climate control turned on in the rare books room, the other rooms don't need it. I was hailed by a neighbour having a good look over the hedge when the builders were here, so I invited her over for a cup of tea and told her the same story – I'm sure the whole neighbourhood's been informed by now.'

Arapera noticed with amusement that even the coffee cups were nineteen-fifties style and was just about to comment, when Fiona exclaimed, 'Sorry! I completely forgot to ask if you got paid properly. Did they pay out your holiday entitlement after all?'

Fiona studied Arapera's face for a moment as if she was trying to decide what to say or maybe how to say it. 'I don't want to invade your privacy, but I thought about this last night and how you went out on a limb to try to push for that software in the meeting – so cleverly done without actually saying anything definite. And if I hadn't asked for the meeting, you wouldn't have taken that risk, so I feel responsible.'

'Oh God, no! It was totally my decision to take the risk, so don't feel you have to help me. I'd made up my mind beforehand that I'd try and push it a bit in front of a client in case it made a difference.'

'But I want to,' said Fiona mildly. 'I really do, and why wouldn't I do it when it's only due to my travel schedule that I can't employ you right away. Just give me your bank account number and I'll set up an AP — do you want to be paid fortnightly or monthly?'

Ten minutes later they stood in the open front door and Arapera said, 'If you send me links to useful web sites, I'll start learning more about the kind of things you sell, so I've got some clues about what I'm handling later on. I mean for next time you go away, if your friend can't come and mind the business.'

Turning her head now and then to catch glimpses of the harbour through the misty rain, Arapera drove down the winding streets towards town and realised that in the last two hours she had not once thought of those two girls she saw, the girls who weren't there. The benefit of distractions, she thought, such amazing revelations and so much to think about that my mind pushed those disturbing thoughts to one side.

Acting on an impulse she did a little circuit in the CBD and drove along Lambton Quay to see if anything would re-emerge in her memory, but nothing happened even though she slowed right down at the point of the accident and looked straight at the marks on the pavement. Maybe I'd need to walk along and stop right where it happened, she thought as she parked in Palmer Street, maybe if I stood there something would trigger that elusive piece of memory.

The Soldierpilotpilot blog (611891 followers)

#coolchick #thequeenofcool

Another pause to our normal agenda, because what's been happening in the last couple of days is the stuff that movies are made about. Something so strange and unexpected that it takes precedence over world affairs.

Social media and the news media have leapt on this latest development like starving wolves; it has created a frenzy of speculation going viral globally and understandably so.

A Mrs Wilson, who worked in the shoe shop that used to be just down the street from where the car nearly killed the Queen of Cool, informed a newspaper that two young girls were killed in that spot by a run-away van with an unconscious man behind the wheel 23 years ago. She said, 'I can point out the exact spot where it happened, and it's within six feet of where that car crashed the other day.'

I'm so gobsmacked by this that I can't think clearly, I feel dislocated from reality. All my previous reference points relating to logic appear to have no relevance today, they've been overwritten by magic. More later, I need a drink. But before I head for the wine bottle, and just because a few of you have asked again: No, I've not given up on writing about climate change and politics and food and my cat and flying (those are the things that I have been asked for assurance about so far), but for the moment I'm so immersed in the saga about the Queen of Cool that I haven't had time to concentrate on other things.

Chapter 19

Arapera was still on the sofa where she had been sitting since six that morning. She couldn't quite rouse herself to get dressed, still tired after a disturbed night, and thought she might just spend the whole morning in her PJs, an act totally out of character. Then her phone buzzed with a call but having read the morning's new blog post from Soldierpilotpilot, she hesitated when she saw that the caller was Carmen, because she knew exactly what she wanted to talk about, and she wasn't sure if she could handle it right then.

'I told you they were ghosts, didn't I?' said Carmen, triumphant to have been right and continued, as if she forgot to think about how Arapera might feel. 'What did they look like? Kind of old-fashioned?'

'Oh, for God's sake – would you stop it!' said Arapera. 'For a start, it's not exciting, it's driving me mad, and I refuse to believe in ghosts, I really do. And why would they look old-fashioned? I was only twenty-three years ago – we were four or five at the time. They looked perfectly normal to me, just two kids with ponytails, dressed in jeans and sweatshirts. And if you don't mind, I'd rather not keep talking about it. The other night was quite enough.'

Hoping to divert Carmen's ghoulish exuberance, she adds. 'What's happening with you and Ollie – he seemed quite cheerful the other night. Are you feeding him happy pills, or something?'

'I don't know what you mean,' said Carmen sounding slightly confused, as if she truly didn't, and it occurred to Arapera that maybe Ollie had never seemed withdrawn and morose to Carmen. Perhaps he was different when they were alone, or worse, perhaps the combination of Carmen and herself made him withdrawn, perhaps their chats bored him.

'Oh, never mind, I've just felt a couple of times lately that he seemed a bit down,' said Arapera now, hoping to retrieve the situation. 'But the other night he was back to normal. I was hoping his new job wasn't getting on top of him or too boring or something.'

The things we say, she thought with slight embarrassment, these social lies and evasions we voice to avoid hurting someone's feelings, recovery lies to retrieve a bad situation. But if Carmen has never thought of Ollie as morose, then who am I to risk making her unhappy – with me or with him?

'I'll tell you something exciting, though, but you have to keep it to yourself.' Carmen was obviously not insulted on Ollie's behalf. 'We're not telling all and sundry for a while yet, in case it goes wrong, you know. But I'm pregnant again – just up to the three months mark now. Would you channel positive thoughts in my direction, please?'

'Oh, lovely! I'm so happy for you.' Arapera was genuinely delighted to hear the news, because the miscarriage a year ago had thrown ebullient Carmen into a very uncharacteristic depression that had worried everyone who knew her. 'I'll think lots of happy thoughts and send them your way every day!'

Their conversation was interrupted by Arapera's phone discretely signalling a string of messages and she excused herself. 'I'll talk to you later, but I'd better check what all these messages are about.'

Ending the call, she looked incredulous at eight text and four Facebook alerts on her screen. Why was this happening, multiple messages from her mother who lived in Blenheim? Nothing like this had ever happened before, and she hesitated to read them. Had her mother found out she had a serious illness, or had she been in an accident or had she caught up with Arapera's accident? Reluctantly Arapera put her finger on the text message icon and scrolled to the earliest of the eight messages.

'Just got engaged, more to follow! Very happy!'

followed by a row of emoticons: two hearts, glass of wine, smiley face and two balloons.

The next message read, 'In love with gorgeous hunk, can't believe how happy we are!' followed by another row of emoticons, four this time.

The third message was, 'Engagement party soonish! You must both come, can't wait to introduce my darling Juan." Followed by another four emoticons.

By the time she had read all eight messages that seemed to have gone to Jackson and herself, she understood a bit more and final one, which said "check FB", followed by three red exclamation marks explained the Facebook alerts.

Heaving a deep sigh, Arapera lay back on the sofa and arranged a cushion under her head before she opened Facebook, took one look and said out loud, 'Oh my God! I don't believe it!'

The first photo in her mother's Facebook post showed a young guy, probably about Arapera's age but maybe a couple of years older, standing between rows of grapevines with a backdrop of distant sun-drenched hills, which she only noticed later, after she had managed to tear her eyes away from the open shirt and the sculpted chest of the man, who clearly spent many hard hours in a gym lifting weights to define his muscles. This was followed by three posts all featuring the same man with and without her mother, both exuberantly smiling and in one, holding glasses of champagne with their arms linked.

Seconds after she had read the messages a second time, Jackson called, his voice a mixture of disbelief and amusement. 'Did you see it yet? Did you see that guy?'

They compared notes and Jackson laughed at Arapera's description of their mother's fiancé as "perfect for the cover of a romance novel".

'I wouldn't know – I don't read those,' he said with a snigger of disdain. 'I'm an army guy - I hate to think what would happen if one of the guys lay on his bed with a book with a cover like that, total disaster, unless it was a fitness manual. But what's she done with her face? And she's got pink streaks in her hair, for God's sake! I can't put my finger on what's so different about her face, but she must have had some kind of treatment - she looks about thirty-five.'

'Yep, she seems to have lost twenty years since I saw her last summer – and she's much slimmer too, did you notice? Obviously, a mid-life change that paid dividends. Wonder if she had a real facelift or if it's Botox?'

Jackson sighed. 'I wouldn't know how to tell the difference, but I suppose as long as she's happy, we shouldn't laugh at her. It's just that I didn't see it coming. I saw her when we went south for that training exercise in the mountains last year, and she didn't look anything like this - and there was no talk of the incredible hunk or any other guy.'

He hasn't heard about the accident yet, thought

Arapera, so maybe it isn't really as widespread as I thought, and he might never learn what happened. Not until she put the phone down and picked up her Kindle, did she realise that she had not heard a single word from her mother about the accident either and thanked her lucky star. And long may it last, she thought, the longer she remains ignorant, the better for my mental state. I need no more excitement.

And as always when she considered her mother, images from her childhood and early teenage years surfaced, and she had to brace herself against the pain of those memories. Her feelings of abandonment when her father punished her and her mother simply left the room, usually the kitchen, and retreated upstairs. And even when she and Jackson moved away with their mother and lived in a flat in Levin, she had never felt she had a bond with her mother, there was no feeling of real affection. Jackson was probably closer to her, but for Arapera there was a void where a mother's concern and protection should have been. Every so often she wondered if they might become closer over time, but she had no idea if her mother felt the same way. Perhaps she had deliberately forgotten the way she walked away from the brutality her father inflicted on Arapera, not just turned away but actually walked away to another part of the house or outside. Or maybe she had re-written the past in her mind and no longer thought that she had failed to protect her daughter. She would never know, of course, because one thing Arapera had got used to from childhood was the code of silence, that nothing about what was done to her was to be talked about with anyone and never referred to with either parent.

And as if conjured up by these memories, and before Arapera had time to post any kind of comment on Facebook, her mother called, taking Arapera by surprise and having to quickly pull herself together, to move from the past to the present so as not to say the wrong thing.

'Hi Mum, how are you? Celebrating I see – congratulations!'

'Oh yes, I'm so, so happy – you can't imagine how happy I am, the happiest in my entire life. I've never known anyone like Juan before. He's just amazing.'

Her mother sounded more cheerful and upbeat that Arapera had ever her sound. It was impossible to reconcile this exuberant exclamation with the mother she recalled from that worst day fourteen years ago, the woman who without comment turned and left her lying on the kitchen floor, and who later said, 'I can't help you, just take a couple of painkillers and go to bed.'

And now, this unexpected transformation had turned her mother into a new person, but one just as hard to fathom as Arapera's memory of her. Even her vocabulary and the way she expressed herself had changed, like a fast forward from the past to the present. The conversation that followed was difficult because Arapera, who was pleased for her mother and wanted to wish her well, found it hard to make her voice enthusiastic enough to sound convincing. They ended the call fifteen minutes later with her mother promising to send an invitation to the engagement party, an event that she promised would be "a mega celebration at the vineyard where I work, and the entire workforce invited".

'I must get over it,' Arapera said to herself. 'I'm a strong person, I should be able to cope and try to forget even if I can't forgive – or understand.'

There had been many beatings, but in her mind, that dreadful day might as well have happened yesterday and not all those years ago, the day when she thought she was going to die, when she truly realised how dangerous it was arguing with her father. When her mother turned her back and didn't intervene, and Arapera lay bleeding on the kitchen floor and accepted that there was nobody who could protect her, and that she must somehow survive until she was old enough to leave home.

But how do you forget a thing like that? she thought, staring at the phone still held limply in her hand. Maybe I can forgive Mum, try to think of reasons why she abandoned me like that when I honestly thought Dad was inches away from killing me. But I was only thirteen, for God's sake and I can't forget it, every detail is clear in my mind.

She put her phone on the sofa and went to get dressed.

The Soldierpilotpilot blog (714356 followers)

#coolchick

#thequeenofcool

Here's a thing — you know how hard it can be to express something perfectly. Like when you're talking to someone or responding to a comment on social media, and then a bit later you think of the perfect reply, the one you didn't think of at the time. Which is infuriating and makes you wish you could rewind time and SAY it, get it right. And it particularly applies when you want to make a pun, or maybe a sarcastic or scathing reply.

But never mind - yesterday on the RNZ morning programme, they were talking about the strange phenomenon of "the two girls who weren't there" with a psychologist, and she made the perfect comment. I've been back to the podcast of the interview to make sure I get the quote right, and this is it, verbatim:

"I don't believe in ghosts, and I don't think she is suffering from delusions or hallucinating. I do believe she saw what she says she saw - which is clearly a contradictory statement, and you could say that I have effectively stated that she experienced a hallucination. But no, I am saying that she did see those girls — that they were momentarily physically there, but only she could see them."

And then this wonderful woman laughed at herself and added: "And now I'll sit back and wait for the New Zealand

Psychological Society to investigate my mental state and maybe de-register me."

So, there you have it. If we can just accept this single unexplainable event without hysteria, scorn or ridicule and without making references to witches or "nutters" then the problem resolves itself. Take it as read, accept it as a random glitch in the time continuum, stop fussing and fuming and get on with life. And most important of all, let the Queen of Cool get on with her life.

Chapter 20

Early in the morning a couple of days later Arapera looked in dismay at the list of callers and the number of message and emails alerts on her phone. Sitting up in bed she scrolled through what had appeared since she turned the phone off the previous afternoon, when she had felt overwhelmed by how much attention was focused on her now, increasing exponentially day by day. Had anything ever been so tiring and so sapping of mental energy? She muted the sound, left the phone face down on her bed and went to have a shower.

Once again sitting sideways in her favourite sofa corner with her bare feet up and her laptop resting on her knees, she steeled herself to open her email account, determined to check every message and either reply or consign them to the spam folder. But what she found surprised her and forced her to face the fact that her privacy was now non-existent, because people she had never heard of had got hold of her email address and so had media.

Thirty-four unread emails. This was a nightmare, far worse than she had predicted when she discussed it with Carter, and they had agreed that a short burst of unwanted fame was probably going to make her life slightly uncomfortable. A momentary temptation to close the laptop and ignore the messages was discarded as unrealistic and she decided she must plow through them and check each one. Half an hour later she had the tally in her head: nineteen were from media, both print and broadcast, seven from friends, five from total strangers and three from family.

She glanced at the gorgeous spring day outside the window and decided that a concerted effort should clear this mass of messages before lunch and then she would go for a long walk or a run to test out how recovered her ankle was. Gazing unseeingly at her feet she considered her options. Obviously, privacy was important but setting up a new email account was no guarantee of being protected from this onslaught of interest. It only took one family member or friend to let a new email address slip, maybe by forwarding a reply from her to somebody else and then she would be right back where she was now.

Reluctantly she set about reading every email right through instead of just checking who sent it, and what she found changed her mood and at times even made her laugh. Most of the media messages were tedious, asking her to reply to a list of questions and send her answers back "to ensure we get the details right", which sounded reasonable in a way, but also left things open for misinterpretation. If she did what they asked, they could say they interviewed her, but they could include speculation about things they had not asked her to comment on, and the result might be very misleading. Some asked her to take part in a recorded interview, which side-tracked her because it might explain the huge number of missed call alerts on her phone, so she went back to the phone and listened to twelve messages, all of which she deleted, and then she returned to the emails.

'Great!' she said out loud and consigned twelve media emails to the spam folder before she continued looking at the seven that remained, which from the way they were worded indicated that the writer presumed she would welcome attention, and they were funnier than those she had got rid of. One radio host wanted her to take part in a discussion panel consisting of a medium, a psychologist and a "ghost hunter" in a Zoom meeting to be broadcast live; she replied politely that she was unavailable. Another asked her to record an interview where the person asking questions would be a popular writer of paranormal romantic fiction, which resulted in another "no" and a question mark in her mind about what made someone think a romance writer was an appropriate interviewer.

How inventive they are, she thought, quite creative and looking at things through different lens than print media, possibly because commercial radio is such a personality focused medium, and the hosts are more interested in bolstering their personal popularity than just reporting facts.

Then she read the fifth of the seven and moaned with dismay; this station had done their research and asked if she would come on their morning program to talk to her father live on air. She felt sick at the mere thought. Meeting him for lunch once in a while when he was in Wellington was something she could to brace herself for and plan how to handle herself to retain control of the conversation. She would prepare diverting topics to use if he got intense and prime herself to remember to keep a straight face, but not completely serious or she would be accused of sulking, just calmly half-smiling. After years of performing this balancing act, she knew she could do it and survive forty-five minutes without disaster but talking to him live on radio or even recorded was out of the question. They might prime him to ask things she would never consent to discuss with him even in private, or they could use his extreme religious beliefs as a trigger to set him raving; anything was possible.

She paused for a moment and wondered how they had made the connection, but probably the combination of her father's reputation for religious fanaticism that had brought him unfortunate media attention in the past and their unusual surname had done it. How could they resist trying to tempt such an enticing father/daughter duo to discuss those girls who weren't there? It was an opportunity they would have tagged as perfect as soon as they read about her father's religious beliefs. There couldn't be many people with the name Woodhill, who regularly stood outside supermarkets with large placards and harassed shoppers with doomsday predictions and warnings about eternal hellfire, so simply Googling her name would have brought up media reports about her father.

The last media email was from the host of a show on a major commercial station, who wanted her to go on air with a well-known and self-designated rationalist to discuss what she had seen, and she nearly said yes. It made her smile to imagine how she would demolish their hoped-for debate in one minute by saying that she couldn't agree more, she didn't believe in ghosts either and she regarded anything paranormal as nonsense. But common sense prevailed, and she declined that offer too without explanations.

Glancing at the time, she wondered if she would be able to reply to the emails from friends and family before lunch, possibly an unrealistic goal, but setting a time limit on doing it would ensure she completed the job, however tedious. The wording and how much to say would take time, and each message must be tailored for the person she was writing to because the last thing she wanted was to create some unwanted impression or use an ambiguous phrase that could be misinterpreted. But in the end, it turned out to be easier than she had first thought, because once she had replied to two of them, she copied and pasted whole paragraphs into other replies with slight changes and completed the task in an hour. I deserve a cup of tea, she thought, and a couple of biscuits because that went so well, and I only have three left now – well, not counting text messages, of course, but voice messages and emails will all have been taken care of.

Jackson's email was predictably short and to the point, and it made her smile to read her younger brother's reaction when he heard that she had apparently seen ghosts: "I thought ghosts didn't came out in daylight, so it must have been a couple of kids who ran off after the crash, don't know why everyone is getting so excited, but people always jump to crazy conclusions. Really glad you didn't get crushed - see you soon. Jackson."

How unusual, thought Arapera, I can't remember when Jackson last sent an email instead of calling or texting, but perhaps he just heard or read about the accident and felt it required a more formal approach. The thought of Jackson pondering a serious way of telling her he's glad she wasn't crushed, made her smile.

The email from her aunt Jean was longer and required some thought before she replied, because Jean was kind and as different from her dad as anyone could be. So typical, thought Arapera, she's mostly concerned about how tiresome this is for me and she worries it will drive me crazy if it continues, but at the same time she's quite intrigued, just as would I be if I read about it happening to someone else. Last of all she read her cousin Rick's entertaining reaction to the news: "I spend so much time in churchyards looking for the graves of ancestors that seeing a few ghosts seems quite reasonable. I hope you really weren't hurt, must say it seems incredible that you didn't get killed. Someone was looking after you, for sure. The video is amazing and lots of people are sharing it here."

Finally, the job was done. With a sigh she closed the laptop and picked up the phone again, only to find more text messages than last time she looked. Thanking fate for giving her a good memory, she scrolled through them and ignored all the ones she had already dealt with via emails, which left a dozen mostly from friends. And nothing from her father, which hopefully meant he had not heard or seen anything more about the accident and might never hear about the ghost girls.

I wish I knew how to recreate the whole sequence of events in my mind, thought Arapera and stared unseeing at the screen. Now that I know about that previous accident and the two little girls, the missing piece has become more enervating than before. I know how Soldierpilotpilot described it, but the tiny piece I crave is what I felt my arm hit or not hit when I pushed the girls aside. Was it something physical, something real or was it just air with no substance?

The Soldierpilotpilot blog (788134 followers)

#coolckick

#thequeenofcool

#revengeforthequeenofcool

Two things this week have come like the proverbial bolt from the blue. The first, but not the most important, is how dramatically my follower numbers have shot up, which is pleasing for my ego. And the second, which should have been number one in order of importance - but I couldn't resist boasting a bit – is the bigamy story that erupted over the weekend. Who would have thought that these diverse factors: my blog, her name being discovered, the videos, the original accident where the two sisters were killed and lots of social media attention etc would conspire to expose a criminal?

It seems incredible, and now that I write it, I think criminal is too bland a word for that devious bastard – let's call a spade a spade: the man is a total shit. Not only because he was married to two people at the same time, but also because he left his (obviously illegal and therefore invalid) marriage to the Queen of Cool, taking with him (in accordance with the Relationship Properties Act) half the value of the apartment she owned. It seems he had nothing much when they married, but she owned a flat already at age 22. And he wasn't entitled to a cent of her money, but he stayed the required three years, so he'd get half of what was hers. I know he would have had the same right even if they hadn't married, as co-habiting gives the same right, but as he married her illegally, he was profiting from a crime, which presumably negates his rights under the Act. Or that's what I think, not yet having consulted a lawyer about it.

So now I'm on the warpath on behalf of the Queen of Cool, and I want to know what this despicable piece of humanity did with her money. And will the courts sell whatever he bought and give the money back to her? And — a horrible thought but necessary — are there more "wives" out there? He is older than she is, so theoretically he's had time to "marry" one or two additional times. I assume there might be such a thing as a serial bigamist, who amasses wealth by stealth and deception and only marries women with financial assets.

Today I'm starting a campaign to find out more (links to my media accounts at the bottom of the page), so please communicate what you find out or know, and I will make sure the police know about it. I will use everything people contribute, documents, facts, links to article and names and then make as complete a file of evidence as I can and hand it over to the authorities. The more detail the better and please don't forget to give me the source and the date for anything significant.

And a message once again for those of you who continue to worry I'm never going to get back to my normal topics: as soon as I've got this bigamy-and-previous-wives-and-stolen-money thing under control, I'll be back to my normal non-drama self.

Chapter 21

An anguished cry from Arapera brought Carter to the living area, half undressed out of his hospital scrubs. 'What's wrong? What happened?'

She was sobbing now with her hands covering he face and for the moment words were beyond her. Carter looked at the phone held limply in her hand, sat down beside her and pulled her against him.

'Come on, girl – it can't be as bad as that, can it?'

'Look!' she sobbed and held the phone out. He kept his arm around her and read the messages on the screen: "One missed call. One voice message" and after a second's hesitation he put the phone to his ear and listened with an expression of disbelief to Arapera's father strident voice. "Arapera! This is urgent! I've seen the video, one of my salesmen has it on his phone, all about the ghosts of those girls. I'm sure you're possessed by a demon again, I'll call you as soon as I know when I can get away for a few hours, just hang on, I'm coming.'

'Oh, shit! We're *not* letting this happen – don't worry, we'll sort it out. We'll make a plan.'

He stopped talking and stayed where he was, with one arm around her, absent-mindedly stroking her shoulder with his unfocused gaze at the window.

'I'm OK now – thanks, Carter.' Slowly she moved away from the comfort of Carters arm and reached for a tissue from the box on the coffee table. 'It just took me by surprise. The tone of his voice brought it all back, and I felt as if I was right back there, lying on the floor with nobody to help me. I kind of forgot about you.' She sniffed, then smiled. 'Not really forget you – I mean, how could I? But in my head, I was thirteen again, back in the kitchen at home.'

Carter looked thoughtful but grim because he knew exactly what she was referring to, and after a few moments he said, 'Would you let me write a text message to him – on your phone? You can press Send yourself if you're OK with it or change it or just delete it. But this is serious, and we've got to put a stop to this asap – we can't have him come barrelling in here threatening hellfire and eternal damnation. I could tell from his voice that he's on a crusade of religious mania again.'

She nodded without speaking and blew her nose before she headed for the bathroom, and Carter picked up his own phone to do some research. When Arapera returned after washing her face with cold water and tying her hair in a ponytail, Carter was pouring glasses of wine.

'Here, take this.' He handed her the bowl of peanuts, picked up their glasses and led the way back to the sofa. 'Now, read this and see what you think,' he said and passed her phone over before he sat down beside her.

"I have taken out an "urgent protection order" against you which will be processed by the court asap. You are not to come within 15 meters of me, not call or message me or in any way attempt to contact me. If you do, I will call the police and you will be arrested."

'Oh God, I never thought I'd ever have to do anything like this,' said Arapera sadly. 'But I really think I must this time. I can't go through that again, I just can't! Thank you! And if I don't do something radical, he'll just keep hounding me or turn up on the doorstep – he never gives up and he gets more aggressive as time goes on if he can't have his way. I'm sorry talking about it always turns me into an emotional wreck.' She lifted the phone and pressed Send.

'Step one completed!' Carter raised his glass in a toast. 'It's a bit early to start drinking wine at half past four in the afternoon, but some days the rules don't apply. And don't worry about what talking about your dad does to you. As I've said many times before, you've been in a state of unresolved post-traumatic stress for over a decade - and how you usually conceal it from people, I truly don't know. You should have had therapy years ago. I'm not a therapist but I'll always be here for you, you know that. So now you have to do the protection order thing for real.'

'What do I have to do? Call the cops?'

'No, no – step two is to go online and actually file the form requesting that a protection order is issued again him. I just quickly read up on it while you were in the bathroom. If he checks what it means, he'll soon know that if he doesn't get the official notification it means you didn't do it.'

'OK, I can do that, but he won't check – he told me recently he thinks the Internet is the work of the devil and those who use it let the devil into their house and he's not going to use it ever again. He's deleted the email app from his phone and he's not using his laptop at all. I wonder how long it's going to be before he realises that he can't get any emails. It was just bad luck that guy showed him the video on his phone.'

Without replying Carter put down his glass and reached for phone. 'I'm just going to check what time Mitre 10 closes tonight – ah, they're open to seven. I'll leave this half glass, put my jeans on and whizz over there and pick up a spy hole for the door. And when I go, you must promise to put the chain on and not open the door even a crack, not for anyone at all till I get back. Or if someone rings the bell you can talk to them through the closed door and find out who it is. OK?'

Her face spoke volumes as she stared at him, eyes wide in disbelief. 'Are you serious? Do you think he might come over here and try to *force* his way in?'

'I wouldn't put it past him. I keep telling you - he's mentally ill, and that in combination with his history of violence means I don't trust him an inch. So, let's be extra careful - it doesn't cost anything, and I'd like to think you're safe when I'm at work. So, we're having a spy hole or peep hole or whatever the heck those things are called.'

'You're probably right,' she said slowly. 'I don't think he's a mental case, but he did nearly kill me that time – he's got a terrible temper. That damn religious extremism fuels his anger, and once he starts raving, he can hardly control himself. I can usually control him, distract him - but now he's on a mission and he'll be more determined than ever. But we haven't got a biscuit cutter.'

'A what?'

And Arapera laughed for the first time since she listened to her father's voice message. 'We need to drill a biggish round hole in the door for that peephole to sit in – that's what they're called, peepholes. Maybe we can check the diameter on the Mitre 10 website – we might just need a very wide drill bit, not a hole cutter.'

'You're the handyman around here, girl - I'll do whatever you say,' said Carter and watched her focused and busy on her phone, looking as if she was getting back to normal now that she had something practical to do. 'And perhaps you should block your dad on your phone too?'

A couple of minutes later she put her phone down. 'Right - we need a half inch brad-point bit for my electric drill, so pick up one of those as well – I know I haven't got one.'

Carter raised his glass in a pretend toast. 'And what would I do without you? I'd probably be reduced to poking a hole in the door with a meat skewer. Drills and what's-it-bits aren't part of my universe. You'd better write it down, so I don't get the wrong thing.'

Just after six Cater put the box with the peephole on the table and handed Arapera the drill bit. 'Great, thank you!' She picked up her electric drill from the kitchen bench. 'I've started dinner, so if you finish it, I'll mount this thing while you do it.'

'No, I'll help,' he said. 'I'll be the security guard – I told you I'm not prepared to take any risks. So, I'll stand halfway down the stairs while you do your thing, and then we'll close that door and you'll be safe whether I'm here or not.'

'Amazing gadget!' said Carter when she had finished, and they were taking turns to check what they could see. 'I hadn't realised it would show such a wide view – I could see the entire width of the landing and halfway down the last flight of stairs.'

'Two hundred degrees it said on the website. I

checked after you left in case some were better than others, but they all seem to be much the same. I'm glad you got one with a steel-coloured rim – somehow, I don't see myself as a girl with a gold-rimmed peephole.'

Carter burst out laughing and made a rude gesture. 'Sound like the title of a porn movie,' he said and went back to the kitchen. 'I'll finish making dinner if you grate some parmesan and get knives and forks out.'

The Soldierpilotpilot blog (879644 followers*)

#revengeforthequeenofcool

#coolchick

#thequeenofcool

As if it wasn't enough being endlessly commented on in media after the bigamy revelation and all the drama and detail that followed, now the Queen of Cool has a following of crazy ghost busters. This is their own description of what they do for a living, apart from one who designates herself as a "spirit cleanser" (which makes me think of alcohol-based household cleaners), who want to use the Queen of Cool to locate the ghosts of crime victims or even bodies.

Enough, you insensitive nutters! Leave her alone! And let's get our combined mental powers to work here, guys – let's all send calming and cheerful thoughts in the general direction of the Queen of Cool. The poor girl must be feeling as if her world is imploding, one damn thing after another. Off the cuff, I can't give you the GPS coordinates, but send kind thoughts towards

Wellington, that will do. And yes, I do understand that sending positive thoughts to someone is not even loosely based on science, but it might make those of us who worry about the Queen of Cool feel better, as if we have done something, however little.

And now for today's exciting development: I've been contacted by a relative of the bigamist who says she'll tell me where he lives (and hopefully where the money belonging to the Queen of Cool is) – provided I pay her $10k first.

What do you think? Should I sell my new mountain bike and pay her? Or is she just an opportunistic liar? Or should I do the obvious thing and call the cops? And then she'll pretend it was just a joke and say she knows nothing, and we're no further ahead.

Chapter 22

Arapera was cleaning the bathroom when Carter called to say he hadn't forgotten it was her birthday and would she please not make any plans for that evening.

'I'm not likely to go anywhere, am I? As you know I hardly dare go outside these days, so I'll be here waiting for the cupcake – and don't forget the candle,' said Arapera and they both laughed, remembering how Carter put a cupcake with a lit birthday candle on her desk at school the day she turned sixteen. The girls in her class had thought it was so romantic, totally convinced by the acted-out romance between them.

She had only just picked up the glass polish again when the phone signalled a new message. She glanced at the screen where a half sentence showed. 'Please call asap…'. A message from Carmen, who hadn't sent anything that sounded so urgent since her miscarriage more than a year earlier. The full text read, "Please call asap, your phone is engaged, must talk NOW!" and Arapera's stress levels rose to new heights.

She called Carmen with her heart beating fast and her mind conjuring up accident scenarios or another miscarriage, but what she heard was so shocking she could hardly breathe for a moment, she felt her chest constrict as if clutched by a large fist.

'It's unbelievable!' exploded Carmen as soon as she answered the call. 'I'm so sorry that he's done this to you, it's unforgivable, he really is mad!'

Then she realised she still had not told Arapera what she was talking about and started again. 'It's your dad – he's just said in an interview on Newstalk ZB that he's convinced you're possessed by a demon, which he's going to exorcise! And he said it's happened before, and you seem to be prone to demonic possession. I mean, he's totally mental, isn't he? This has to stop - what can we do?'

'Nothing,' said Arapera after a pause to give herself time to think. Instinctively she decided to not reveal that her father had already contacted her, or what she and Carter had done about it. To prolong Carmen's outrage and her obvious need to discuss it would only upset Arapera herself further. 'There's nothing *anyone* can do. He truly believes these extreme things, and I'll just stay well away from him. I've blocked him on my phone already and I'll not let him in if he comes to the flat.'

'Ollie thinks you should take out a protection order or whatever it's called, you know, so he can't come within ten metres of you and can't call you or anything. You mustn't let him near you, Arapera! I truly think he's dangerous – next time he starts in on this exorcism stuff you might not survive.'

After a long pause, Arapera said, 'I think I'm safe as long as I stay here and don't go out – and I resigned from my job, so he won't be able to catch me by waiting outside the office. I'll just stay indoors, and I won't answer the door if he comes to the flat.'

It only took her a couple of minutes to find a recording of the interview when they ended the call, and when she did, she knew that Carter had been right in his assessment of what her father might do, and the risk she would expose herself to if she met with him or let him into the flat. He was in full flight, quoting the bible and saying he would rid her of the demon by using "the power of the finger of God" and much more that she could not bear to listen to. She got as far as the mention of the finger of God and knew she would start to cry if she heard the rest. That phrase had the power to put her right back to age thirteen, to that ghastly day.By the time Carter came home from work, she had her feelings under control and managed to tell him about the interview quite calmly, adding, 'If you find it online, please don't play it aloud – I've listened to some of it, and I've heard the rest of it from Carmen.' To change the expression on Carter's face she added, 'And Fiona sent an email and said she'll be in Australia for a bit longer than planned, because it's an opportunity she can't miss – her friend from Napier is happy to stay longer, so Fiona is going to continue her quest into another state and cover twice as much ground as she normally does in a trip. Which means I can just stay inside and not go out at all.'

'I can cover the expenses for two months,' said Carter casually. 'I never spend all my income – the only expensive stuff I buy is good food and shoes.'

Arapera rolled her eyes at herself. 'Sorry! There's no need for you to do that - I forgot to tell you. Fiona's already paying me. Amazing woman – she said it's because she can't employ me right away and I had to resign. She said she feels partly to blame, which is nonsense of course, bit she convinced me to accept. And meanwhile she'll be sending me links to interesting web sites every now and then, if I feel like learning more – you know, if I want to know more about silver and crystal and maybe even signs. I must remember to show you her websites now that I know how to find them – they're so interesting.'

Carter pointed at the three bags he had just put on the bench. 'OK, that's great, but right now I'd like some help to prepare for your birthday party.'

'Birthday party? Isn't it just you and me?' And then she looked at the kitchen bench and what he was unpacking. 'Good lord, Carter! How many people have you invited? That's heaps of stuff – and so much juice and wine!'

'Only a few, just those that matter, but Jackson can't come, he's stuck in his barrack. Come on, they'll be here at six for drinks and then dinner – and we've got to set it up. Pizzas will be delivered at half past seven. I didn't want it to start too late, because most of us have to go to work in the morning, particularly me.'

While Carter changed his clothes, she set out pre-dinner snacks and glasses, tidied away their various items of clothing draped over the back of the armchair they never used and went to change out of her track pants. But no matter how much she kept busy, in the back of her mind fear crouched like a beast waiting to leap.

Dressed in jeans and the black T-shirt with a bandoleer of bullets printed diagonally across the chest that had arrived by courier from Jackson that morning, Arapera returned to the living area. The doorbell went just as Carter turned around and started to laugh at the sight of her, and she could feel his eyes following her as she went to open the door. He was probably dying to remind her to check the peephole, but he managed to restrain himself, and she smiled to herself as she looked through it.

'Happy birthday!' exclaimed Carmen and hugged her, still holding a bunch of flowers in one hand and a parcel in the other. 'Are you surprised? I'm glad to see you got yourself one of those.' She let go of Arapera and pointed the flowers at the peep hole. 'Very good idea.'

'How about you two move a bit further in,' said Ollie from behind her. 'We shouldn't be standing here with the door wide open if she's in danger, should we? Cool T-shirt!'

'My dad doesn't have the code for the street door, 'said Arapera, 'but people have been known to follow someone else in and appear at our door without warning. I think he did it once, so not what I want right now.'

'This is so great - I haven't had a birthday party for years. Just what I needed!' said Arapera quietly to Carter an hour later and looked around the room where their eight guests were talking and laughing. 'And I can't imagine how you managed to get hold of them. You don't have their phone numbers, do you? And even Thomas and Bugsy!'

'Can't you imagine? Really?' Carter laughed. 'I just checked the contacts on your phone, of course. Don't forget we gave each other our PINs when I first moved in. I can't remember the reason, but thankfully you hadn't changed it. And your former team was easy, I just called the office yesterday and talked to them.'

Much later, after pizza, more wine and lots of

laughter, mostly caused by Henderson, who had been Arapera's running mate for several years and was an irrepressible party show-off, his wife Justine returned from the hall with a cardboard box.

'Happy Birthday!' she said and deposited the box on Arapera's lap. 'But I think we need to clear the table - and get some plates.'

The cake that came out of the box was shaped like an oversized running shoe and iced in the exact colours of Arapera's favourite shoes.

'What an amazing cake! Did you make it?'

'She's been going to a cake decorating class all year,' said Henderson proudly. 'I don't think I really understood before how creative it is – an art form. Last month she made a backpack cake for my brother, who loves hiking.'

'Too special to cut up and eat,' said Carter. 'Let's have the one I bought and hid in my bedroom instead. I can't bear to think of this one getting ruined.'

'Don't be silly!' said Justine. 'I can make another one next year, so long as you send me a new photo of her shoes – she's sure to have a new pair by then. And I've taken photos of this one that I'll forward to you, so you have a memento if you want one.'

I was just after midnight when Arapera started the dishwasher and gave the kitchen bench a final wipe.

'All done – and thank you for organising this! A

whole evening with ten of us and not a single word about the girls who weren't there – did you warn them not to talk about it?'

'It was more like an ultimatum,' said Carter and shunted the sofa back to its normal position. 'Either keep off the topic or get asked to leave – your choice. I wasn't going to have your party turn into some tormenting session to satisfy anyone's curiosity.' Then he laughed and added, 'I think Thomas and Bugsy were itching to discuss it though – seeing the story only came out after you had left your job. At one stage Thomas was just about to say something, but I gave him a look, so he stopped.

The Soldierpilotpilot blog (901233 followers)

#revengeforthequeenofcool

#coolchick

#thequeenofcool

So here it is, the explanation of how the bigamist was unmasked, a story of many parts, and also of coincidence, or maybe we should call it providence intervening in an unexpected way.

Joanne in Pukekohe shared the story about the accident and the aftermath on her Facebook page, one of the stories that had the Queen of Cool's real name. And then Kerrie, a friend of the Queen of Cools mother, who was a at the wedding of the Queen of Cool and the bigamist, saw Joanne's post that somebody shared and added a photo from the wedding in a comment. And by various twists and turns that photo got shared another three or nine times and came to the notice of Gregory in Hobart, who in turn shared it and tagged his sister Wendy and said, 'Hey, Wendy, isn't this your absent husband?' And it was. He and Wendy separated but never divorced due to a disagreement about who should have custody of a horse. And then this thorough bastard came to live in New Zealand and "married" the Queen of Cool.

So now I'm suddenly internationally famous for the Queen of Cool rescue mission - more than for any controversial/entertaining subjects I have blogged about. The traffic on my social media accounts (same name as the blog, links at the bottom of the page) has increased a hundred-fold, if not a thousand-fold, which is how I was able to track how the info spread to Gregory in Tasmania. People are offering to help with the rescue/revenge in various ways, everything from providing funds to some, who live in Australia, offering to find the bigamist. One has offered to kill him - which we obviously don't want. Let him live so we can get her money back and then continue to name, shame and torment him.

Not only has the strange circumstances around what the Queen of Cool saw at the accident scene caught the attention of media here, but it's being shared all over the globe it seems. Those videos are on YouTube of course — and so are some additional things people have turned into videos, like images from the archives of the newspaper reports of the original accident (the one where the two little girls were killed).

I am making progress with my research and pulling together what people send me about the bigamist and the file is becoming very detailed and interesting, soon to be handed over to the cops. I might have to turn it into a book — no, only kidding, I would never do anything to embarrass the Queen of Cool, but I have to admit it would make a great TV drama.

Tonight, I'm doing something that's possibly a bit risky, and I might end up with my nose bloodied or a black eye, but I can't tell you until tomorrow. But I will tell you, whether it goes wrong or turns out OK. Fingers crossed

Arapera looked up from her Kindle. 'Did you just say something? I was deep in this book, and I didn't pay attention.'

'No reason why you should pay attention to me when you're reading. But yes, I said that I've been trying to find out who this Soldierpilotpilot really is, but I haven't got anywhere yet. Which might be because he's really great at keeping himself anonymous or – more likely – because I'm not very good at IT things. I reckon you should try. You know all the tricks and I'd really like to know more about him.' Carter frowned. 'I saw him in one of those videos lying beside the car and though he got up a couple of times to talk to the rescue guys, he never turned around, so I don't even know what he looks like. Thick brown hair, nice jeans and a neat bum is all I have to go on.'

She considered his face for a moment and tried to

imagine why he was so intent on this quest of his. He had mentioned it before, but why was he doing it? Had she inadvertently revealed how often she thought of Liam since the accident?

'I don't think it matters *who* he is,' she said slowly. 'It's *what* he is that matters, an amazingly kind and together sort of guy. A bit like you, actually. He was so good for my state of mind while I was stuck under that car – just so normal and calm and undramatic. And his blog is great, clever and focused. It's kind of like having a mentor or an adjudicator working on my behalf. You know, tempering the extremist views, being sensible – filtering the madness.'

'Yeah, I know, but I'd still love to know more, including where that name comes from. I thought I might post a question on his blog, but I searched through the section called "frequently asked questions" on his website the answer he gives is "I just thought it sounded good" which is a load of bollocks. There's got to be a reason for a name that crazy.'

'I don't care one way or the other, but good luck! I had a message from Jackson while you were at work, and I've asked him to come down for a visit – he's got a couple of days off, so I said he can camp here, and I'll get to have some time with him. Hope you don't mind if he turns up tonight?'

'God no, of course not. I haven't seen him for ages, and it makes up for not having him here at your birthday party. And talking about that – those guys from your old team really rate you, don't they? Couldn't stop telling everyone how marvellous you are and how you never lose your cool. And of course, they didn't just say that - they referred to you as their Queen of Cool.'

He laughed at her expression and changed the subject. 'And what are you reading, anyway? Something interesting?'

'That book you recommended a few weeks ago - Before You Knew My Name. It's very good, which is why I didn't hear what you said. It's so beautifully written, just as you said when you read it, and the story is mesmerising. Best book I've read for ages.'

'When is Jackson arriving? If he's going to be here in time for dinner, we'd better check what we have in the fridge that's enough for three.'

'We can have pasta with crushed tomatoes and a dozen meatballs that I took out of the freezer, and we have parmesan - and lots of ice cream from the birthday party because you forgot to get it out when Justine brought that cake out.'

'I'm really pissed off with dad now,' said Jackson that evening. 'I usually get on with him but apparently, he said in public that mum's a depraved sinner and a whore, and now it's on social media, bloody unbelievable. Thanks to you.'

'Thanks to me!' exclaimed Arapera, completely

taken aback. 'I would never put anything like that on social media or even mention it. What's it got to do with me?'

'I don't mean that you did anything, but it's like anything to do with our family now is of interest after your accident – or after you saw those ghosts. But dad's totally out of order, it's *not* OK to say that about your children's mother. I called him when I first discovered it and said I'll have nothing to do with him until he apologises in public – like on Twitter or something.'

Arapera stared fascinated at her little brother, who was scowling ferociously at nothing in particular and seemed ready to start a public fight with their father.

'Heavens, Jackson – I've never seen you so angry with dad before. I know it's awful, and I hadn't caught up with the depraved woman comment yet, but you know he's a bit crazy, right? Think of what he said in that radio interview the other day.'

'What interview? Don't tell me he's been on bloody radio spouting insults at mum!'

Carter, who had sat silently listening and watching Jackson get more and more wound up, intervened and said decisively, 'Listen mate, there's stuff you haven't heard yet and it's only going to make you angrier, so if I tell you, it's on the condition that you don't go on and on about it and upset Arapera further. She's had just about all she can take at the moment.'

He glanced at Arapera who was trying to imagine how the boys could discuss anything without her being part of it, when Carter said, 'You and I will go outside for a few minutes and leave Arapera to tidy up our plates and serve up some ice cream and whatever she can find. Come along!'

He led the way and Jackson followed, then she heard the door close and their footsteps on the stairs, and she stayed where she was, wondering how much Carter would tell her brother, who had never heard about the exorcism. She didn't mind him knowing, but she would never talk to him about it herself. At the time he had been too young, only ten, and she had felt certain that neither parent would tell him, so if she didn't mention it, he was safe from the knowledge of what went on that day.

She thought back to how she had worn a jumper for several days to hide the wounds on her arms, though it was far too warm, just like she had done several times before so Jackson wouldn't ask questions. He had noticed that the edge of the kitchen vinyl had lifted and that the carpet in the doorway to the dining room was damp, and she could hear her father's voice now, casually telling Jackson when he got back from camp how the water connection under the sink had come loose and what a job it had been to mop up the resulting flood.

When the doorbell finally rang and she went to let them in, she had cleared up in the kitchen and got dessert ready, but all the time she had worried about how Jackson would react. Probably Carter would play the interview back to him and then talk him through the background, but would he actually tell him any details? And if he did, how much? The last thing she wanted was for Jackson to confront their father and cause a fight or an argument in public.

Jackson took one step inside the door and put his arms around her, and she could hear from his voice that he'd been crying. 'Why didn't you tell me? Why did you leave me out of it? I would have helped you, gone to the cops or something, told auntie Jean. And mum standing there doing nothing – it's incredible, I can't believe how you coped. You should have told me!'

She held him to her and stoked his back. 'I was trying to protect you, because you were so young, only ten - far too young to confront trauma like that. Now come and sit down, darling.'

Arapera liberated herself from his grasp and went back to the living room. 'Let's have some tiramisu ice cream, it's delicious, and we can talk while we eat it.'

'Not that I don't want to punch him,' Jackson said, disgusted and still angry after a long talk. 'But Carter's right – the focus would be on you again and that's not good. I wish it had been reported at the time though. Why didn't you?'

'I might have if I'd thought that mum would back me up. And though I was only thirteen I realised that reporting him for assault and mum saying it hadn't happened could be a disaster for me, so I said nothing. I did tell auntie Jean a bit, not the whole thing of course, and she showed me a letter she had kept for years. And once I read it, I knew I'd made the right decision.'

'What was the letter about?'

'It was from our grandfather, dad and auntie Jean's father. He wrote it to her when she was twenty and had just left home, when she said something to dad, and he beat her up one night outside granddad's house. She'd gone home to have dinner with her parents and dad was there too, he'd left home a few years before her. They left together and she had a go at him about how he had talked to grandma over dinner, so he beat her up, broke her cheekbone and left her lying in a puddle of blood. Granddad drove her to hospital, and then the next day he wrote her a letter."

She looked from Jackson to Carter and moved her head slowly from one side to the other, still finding it hard to believe. 'Imagine this – in the letter granddad said he didn't want Jean to do anything about it, to not report it or talk about it, because dad had just started going out with our mum at the time, and he thought she would be good for him and help him control his temper and grow up. Imagine! He'd been physically fighting with Jean all through their teenage years, and she's so much smaller and four years younger, and now their dad asked her not to report a serious assault. I suppose our grandparents never saw dad's temper after he followed mum when she returned to New Zealand, they only came for a visit once or twice. And then auntie Jean immigrated too, perhaps she did it to keep an eye on dad, as if she felt responsible. And sometimes I've wondered if our grandparents put up with dad's violence because they lived in a small town up in Scotland and belonged to a very strict chapel, and they would have been shamed, as they say, if it had come out.'

'Jesus! You never told me this,' said Carter. 'So, Jean didn't mention it to your mother? Didn't warn her about the guy she was about to marry?'

'I think she was scared of retaliation.' Arapera paused. 'And it shows you, doesn't it, what not speaking up and keeping secrets does – it perpetuates the damage. And I think it's definite that dad never assaulted anyone who isn't a family member, though that's poor comfort. He's never got into a fight even with people who argue with him about his doomsday signs outside the car yard – he gets very worked up and shouts, but he's never hit anyone, I don't think.'

'And on the other hand,' said Carter, 'if Jean had warned your mum and she hadn't married your dad, then you two wouldn't exist – and you don't have a violent streak either of you, so the cycle is broken. Do you think Jean still has that letter?'

'I have it now. She said she'd held on to it for years and years and now it was for me to keep.' Arapera hesitated for a moment before she continued. 'When

Jean gave it to me she said I should keep it "as insurance'- I didn't ask what it might be insurance against, but I could tell she felt very strongly about it, so I promised I would.'

When they eventually went to bed, she was emotionally exhausted, but Jackson was calm again and accepted that letting sleeping dogs lie and not confronting their parents was the better option right then, rather than causing an uproar with Arapera potentially being exposed to more media attention. He took the bedding Arapera handed him, gave her a one-armed hug and turned to make a bed for himself on the sofa.

The Soldierpilotpilot blog (967312 followers)

#revengeforthequeenofcool

#coolchick

#thequeenofcool

This post has had to wait its turn because I had to leave my secret lair and go into town and hand over my evidence folder regarding the bigamist to the cops. And I must state here and now that we are damn lucky to have the kind of police force that we have. While I waited to be seen (I had not made an appointment) I was taken behind the first line reception desk to a waiting room, which I shared with a couple of interesting individuals, one of them quite loud and impatient. He eventually got abusive and threatened violence, and the way this was dealt with was a textbook example of perfect, calm de-escalation. So good on you, thin blue line, it was a pleasure to watch how well it worked.

Now, about my slightly risky venture last night. Here's what I did, from A to Z: I went online a couple of days ago and researched the bigamist's relative (female) who contacted me with the 'never to be repeated' offer of giving me info about that bastard's whereabouts in return for me paying her 10k (in cash). I found her on a variety of social media and called her from my secondary phone after finding her number on her FB page (which was totally devoid of any privacy safeguards).

I lied through my teeth — this is allowed under the "needs must" provision in my life manual — and said I was FB friends with some of hers, named the ones I had selected because they had large numbers of friends (432 and 318 respectively), and said I'd seen photos of her and wondered if she'd be up for a date. She said she's also on Tinder, and we could have talked there, but I told her I'm not on Tinder (true).

We met for a drink last night and I had prepared my strategy. I pretended to get a text alert (which she didn't hear because of the noise in the bar) and took the opportunity to turn the recording function on, put the phone on the table between us and started the charm offensive (yes, I do know how to be charming, though I've never used it to deceive anyone before).

We progressed rapidly to a slightly flirtatious stage, helped by my date rapidly downing her first drink and starting in on the next one, getting friendlier by the minute. Then I introduced the intriguing subject of the 'the two girls who weren't there' as a random bit of interesting news to chat about and she lit up like a Christmas tree — very keen to expound on how strange it was that she "happened to know someone, who knew someone else, who was related to the bigamist and might know where he was now". I then brought up the Soldierpilotpilot blogger and said, "You might not know, but the person who knows where the bigamist lives is mentioned in that blog and I read about it only this morning, what a coincidence".

The lady had by this stage had two glasses of chardonnay and three drinks of rum and coke (because this gossipy relationship took time to develop) and she hadn't eaten any of the bar snacks provided, so she was getting very chatty. She was finding it hard to keep track of her pronouns, alternating between talking about "the person who knows" and "I" and "they".

And then, to my huge surprise, she took my hand across the table and swore me to silence (those were her exact words, and I have respected that promise and not repeated a word of this out loud to anyone) and confessed that she herself is the person related to the bigamist. He is her second cousin, and she knows he's in Australia and lives in Southport in Queensland. She also told me that he's in regular contact with his mother, who lives in Taupo. It never occurred to the lady that I might be the blogger she hopes to get 10k from.

Which means I now know his real name, who his mother is, and where both of them live - great score for the price of a few drinks.

So, there I was first thing this morning waiting to inform the police and to give them a USB stick with a copy of the recording from the bar, the lady's name and all the other material people have provided (considerable amounts) neatly collated into a pretty impressive file. Duty done – thanks everyone! This has been a *shining example of strangers cooperating for a good cause, not just to stop a bigamist but hopefully also with the same objective that motivated me: the wish to achieve something good for the Queen of Cool.*

And here's a shout-out to the bigamist's second cousin, my date last night. Sorry to deceive you and not pay 10k for the info, but if you were prepared to share it with a guy you met for the first time last night, and about whom you know nothing (and no, I'm not called Jerry), then I think asking 10k was a bit greedy. Over and out.

Chapter 24

It was only five minutes after Arapera pulled her jeans on, after a lazy morning on the sofa with a second cup of coffee and her Kindle that the entrance phone buzzed in the kitchen.

'Flower delivery for Woodhill.'

She pressed the door release and checked the peephole when footsteps stopped outside her door; a middle-aged woman holding a bouquet wrapped on elaborate layers of paper.

'Congratulations!' she said exuberantly, when Arapera opened the door and reached for the flowers. 'I'm Lulu – we've selected you for our lead item in tonight's 'This week in Wellington' show. Can we come in?'

That's when Arapera noticed a man holding a phone up high behind the widely smiling Lulu and started pushing the door shut, but now Lulu had her right foot against the door jamb and half her body leaning in.

'Would you please move aside — right now,' said Arapera firmly and tried to force the door shut, but Lulu held her ground and with the smile still on her face tried to push further in, so Arapera used the flowers she was holding as a weapon. With one hand she pushed them hard against the woman's face, and with the other she shoved the door against Lulu's body. Taken by surprise Lulu took a stumbling step back, and Arapera slammed the door shut and put her eye to the peephole. Lulu was looking furious and said something to the man, who came closer and for a moment they stood there studying his phone before they started down the stairs.

At the end of the afternoon Carmen texted "Great move! Love the self-control, no glaring angry face, totally in control, awesome!", followed by a link to YouTube. Arapera leaned against the living room windowsill with the spring sun warm on her back and considered for a moment before she clicked on the link. On the one hand she wanted to see it, obviously the scene when that woman tried to force herself in, but on the other hand it might just add to the despondent feeling she felt when she read the headlines on her laptop over breakfast. Newspapers had dug up archived material about the accidents twenty-three years ago when the two girls were killed, and photos of the scene and social media were still full of speculation and theories.

But the YouTube video made her smile, and she played it twice, because it made her feel better than she had felt for several days. There she was, looking calm and tidy in her bright red T-shirt and her hair in a topknot, listening to the introduction and asking Lulu to get out of the way, then the lightning-fast push with the bouquet of flowers, Lulu stumbling back and the door closing. How on earth did I manage that? she thought. No change of expression, no raised voice, just a firm request to step back and the flowers being pushed into that woman's face. And Carmen's comment was so accurate, I do look like someone in complete control, no sign of how outraged I felt at the time. At least I got some lovely flowers as compensation, discounting the four that broke their stems.

She texted back, "Don't know how you get hold of all these things so fast, must spend your life on your phone. And my face was no reflection of what went on in my mind at the time! All this noise about ghosts makes me feel traumatised on behalf of the poor parents of those girls long ago. Their deaths are being used as click-bait, disgusting!"

Carter's grin when he noticed the flowers that night told Arapera that he had seen the video already.

'Nice work!' he said and dropped a shopping bag on the floor. 'But would you please not go on the

Internet for a while? Or if you do, just read Soldierpilotpilot's blog – nothing else!'

'Why? What have you seen?' She got to her feet with apprehension ramping up to a new high and her hand reached for her phone, but Carter came around the table and took hold of her arm. 'Don't – I'll tell you what it is, I'm sorry it came out so badly. Someone has published images of your mum and the young stud with a lot of snide and supposedly funny comments, and it's being shared so you're bound to come across it.'

He let go of her arm and took the phone out of her hand. 'Come with me and see what I got – more tiramisu ice cream. I whizzed down to Moore Wilson's because we ate all of it when Jackson was here, and I thought we deserved some self-indulgence to compensate for all this shit.'

Sitting together quietly reading and eating tiramisu ice cream was the perfect antidote for stress and dramatic media attention, but Arapera noticed out of the corner of her eye that every now and then Carter put his book down and picked up his phone, only to put it down again a few moments later.

'What *are* you doing?' she asked finally. 'Expecting a vital message? Another date coming up?'

He laughed and looked a bit embarrassed. 'I keep watching the video of you getting rid of that Lulu woman – so cool the way you reacted straight away. And I can't believe they posted that video on their

FaceBook page – you'd think she would rather forget about having been beaten back so cleverly.'

The Soldierpilotpilot blog (1003592 followers)

    #revengeforthequeenofcool

    #coolchick

    #thequeenofcool

Rest assured that the article in the weekend paper had nothing to do with me. I wouldn't stoop so low as to use someone's personal and traumatic life situation to increase the numbers of my followers.

So, let's get back to normal life and leave the Queen of Cool alone to recover, and instead we will talk about the vaccination statistics. The number of people I know who have changed their minds about vaccinations, now that Covid is three years in the past, is amazing. Now you can get the annual flu vaccination with inbuilt Covid booster which will be updated every year in case a new variant emerges, and people clamour for it, even many who used to claim Covid was a myth invented by some mysterious world cabal.

It is about time some common sense returned, though I'm not hopeful it will last. The people who reside in the swamp of magic and conspiracy theories, and who distrust science and authority, will undoubtedly find another issue to engage with. One can only hope that natural selection filters them out over the next few thousand generations.

Chapter 25

Arapera put the vacuum cleaner away, emptied the mop bucket and drank a glass of water before she returned to her corner on the sofa to read the emails she had ignored that morning, when a fit of guilt about the state of the flat overcame her.

"My two girls" was the subject line on the last email, and the sender's name told her all she needed to know: Caroline Hudson, the mother of the two girls who had been killed in that accident twenty-three years ago.

She hesitated to open it, but after a moment she told herself it couldn't possibly be any worse than a lot of other things she had endured lately, and maybe she could help this poor woman in some way. The way the message was worded reminded her of the letters she used to get from her grandparents in Scotland when she was a little girl, somehow formal and friendly at the same time. She pictured Mrs Hudson sitting at her laptop that morning while Arapera cleaned, agonising over her choice of words and hesitating before sending it.

"Dear Arapera,

You don't know me but the two shadows from the past you saw in Lambton Quay, when you were nearly hit by that car, were my daughters, Gemma (10) and Serena (8). I had taken them out of school for an appointment with the orthodontist, and it was nearly the same time of the day as your accident.

I would love to meet you and talk to you if you have time. I know you have been exposed to a lot of attention, but I wouldn't take up a lot of time and I promise not to pester you in future.

Kind regards, Caroline Hudson."

Arapera put the laptop on the coffee table and tried to imagine what she could possibly tell Mrs Hudson and couldn't think of anything realistic. She had only the briefest impression of the two girls, and though she had tried to conjure up more detail since the day of the accident, the memory remained the same. Two young girls in jeans and sweatshirts, both with ponytails, nothing more. After considering her options, she replied and said that due to all the attention focused on her, she was reluctant to meet in a café, but she would be happy for Mrs Hudson to come to the flat for a coffee or a cup of tea.

Having written the message, she debated for several minutes if she should mention how little she had to tell but decided that perhaps the girls' mother would be comforted by just meeting her anyway.

She added her address and phone number, sent it and went to empty the washing machine. Only a couple of minutes later she heard the ping of an email and leaving one of Carter's T-shirts on the edge of the basin she returned to the living room, instantly wanting to know if Mrs Hudson had replied.

"Thank you so much!" wrote Caroline Hudson. "Could I come this afternoon? I'm a relief teacher and from tomorrow I have work for a fortnight, so I can't come into town during the day."

Arapera replied that she would be welcome and looked around thinking how lucky it was that she had just finished cleaning and tidying the whole flat, so she didn't need to hide any mess. When the doorbell went, she checked the peep hole and opened the door for Mrs Hudson, who was recognisable from the newspaper photos from twenty-three years ago that had cropped up on social media in the last few days. Not much older than my mother, thought Arapera, but she looks her age, which probably isn't surprising considering the grief she has lived through.

'I hope this isn't too much trouble,' said Caroline Hudson when Arapera showed her into the living room. 'I was surprised you were at home, because I got the impression from all I've read that you were in your lunch hour when the accident happened, but maybe I got that wrong. I was in town already just now, so I sent the email from my phone just on the off chance that you could come out for coffee in a break - but letting me come to your home is very kind.'

'It's the least I could do,' said Arapera and then wondered what she meant by that random phrase. 'Would you like a coffee, Mrs Hudson? Oh, good – how do you take it?'

'Please, call me Caroline – no need to be formal,' said Mrs Hudson and Arapera nearly expected her to continue and say, "not when you know my daughters".

When Arapera put their mugs on the coffee table there was a short silence, as if neither of them quite knew how to start. But someone had to, so she said, 'How can I help you? There's so little to tell because it happened so quickly, in a split second – there was very little time to notice much at all.'

'Oh yes, I've seen the video – my husband and I have watched it dozens of times.' She gave Arapera a wry smile. 'Sometimes when I press start, I nearly expect to see them there – to see what you saw, I mean. But of course, what we see is only that *you* see them and try to push them out of harm's way.'

'I know, I've watched it over and over too – it's easy to picture just where they were when I saw them, just a step ahead of me.' Arapera hesitated about how far she should go, but Caroline seemed completely calm, though there was a slightly unnerving look on her face when she said that she nearly expected the video to show the actual girls, as if she really meant it.

'I saw the car coming towards me, very fast, and I saw two girls just a step ahead of me and slightly to my left. I hadn't noticed them before that moment, but there they were, and I was sure the car would hit both them and me.' She hesitated for a moment, uncertain about how describe it. 'There was no thought involved, it was just an instant reaction to do that side-step and try to push them back, out of harm's way.'

'Oh yes, I can picture it in my mind,' said Caroline, still composed, and sipped her coffee. 'It's very clear in the video, but I just wondered if there was anything you could tell me, something we can't see. Like what they looked like – I've always wondered, and I still do, if they were terrified, if they realised the danger? Sometimes that thought torments me at night and I get up and do something practical to snap out of it - ironing or dusting, something mindless, rather than lie in bed and think about it.'

It would be so easy to lie and give this woman some comfort, thought Arapera sadly, to say the girls' heads were turned towards each other, that they were laughing and didn't see the car. But she found she couldn't do it, not even as a kindness, though it broke her heart to tell it the way it really happened.

'I'm so sorry, but I can't say what they saw or if

they realised - I didn't see their faces at all. I hadn't noticed them until I was just that one step behind them, and the car came at us.'

Caroline was regarding her with a look of compassion, seemingly quite calm. 'Did they have ponytails?'

'Yes, they both did - one was a bit blonder, and her ponytail was longer I think, and they were dressed in sweatshirts and jeans. I think the taller girl had a mint green sweatshirt and the younger a pink one.'

Caroline's voice was steady when she replied, but Arapera saw tears pooling in her eyes, just about to overflow. 'That's exactly what they were wearing, the sweatshirts were new that week - they agonised endlessly about colours when we bought them. But the taller was the younger one, Serena, she took after me. I was always taller than all my friends at school.'

She paused and they sat there looking at each other without knowing what to say next. Caroline's tears were still threatening to overflow and Arapera was on the verge or crying herself, and then Caroline said with utter conviction.

'You were meant to save them! I know you were only a little girl at the time, but it's as if you and they were just a bit out of step in time, out of synch as my husband says - and *had* you coincided, you would have saved their lives. It was such a marvellous, brave thing to do, and it annoys me that nobody has said that. You risked your life to save them, and it doesn't matter if they were alive or ghosts. My husband feels exactly the same, and he has pointed it out in comments on social media time and time again.'

'Thank you!' said Arapera and wiped her eyes with her fingers. 'I never thought of it like that, but in a way you're right, we were out of synch and in another life, I might have saved them. I'm so glad you believe me - that I saw them, I mean. I hadn't mentioned what colours they were wearing to anyone.'

'Oh, I never doubted you for a moment, and that's exactly what they were wearing that day. My husband said to ask you what colours their tops were, because it was never mentioned in any of the newspaper reports at the time, and it would prove beyond doubt that you really saw them.' She turned the mug in her hands, lost in thought for a moment. 'They were in front of me, about ten metres I suppose. I'd stopped for a couple of moments to look in a shoe shop window, so I was looking at the girls from behind as I hurried to catch up with them, and I was thinking that I must get a new pair of jeans for Gemma - hers were getting too short. Do you believe in ghosts?'

'I never did before, but this has overturned my ideas. I don't know what I think now.'

'Neither do I,' said Caroline decisively. 'I've always scoffed at stories about ghosts and supernatural things. But we must accept that you saw *something*, whatever you want to call it – ghosts or apparitions. I say to people that I think you saw shadows of the past.'

She looked down for a moment, hesitating, and Arapera could see the moment she decided to continue. 'I saw it happen, of course, and that moment lives with me every day and often in my dreams. I don't expect that anything can change that – the horror of seeing your children being crushed to death right in front of you is impossible to describe. I went a bit crazy for a time afterwards and I had to take medication that made me feel terrible, but in a different way. But time has passed and though I can never erase that image from my mind, I think I've learnt to live with it in a strange way. It's become more abstract in my mind, as if I'm remembering the memory, not the actual accident. It was only when I saw the video that it became real and immediate again – but I'm so glad I saw it.'

Caroline put her mug on the table and got to her feet, and Arapera knew there was nothing she could say, no words could express what she felt, so she got up too and put her arms around Caroline, and they remained like that for what seemed like minutes before Arapera dropped her arms and Caroline left after only a few words of thanks.

Chapter 26

After a night of broken sleep with worries swirling in her mind and vivid nightmares, Arapera woke exhausted in the morning to find a text message from an unknown number on her phone. She sat up bleary-eyed and stared at it, reluctant to open the message in case it was another instance of someone crazy fired up with mystic frenzy wanting her to do or try something. But it might also be something comforting like that unsigned message from a different unknown number yesterday that read, "We're not all crazy, hold your head up and ignore them, it will stop eventually" followed by a heart and a thumbs up emoticon.

She opened the message folder, thinking that maybe the best thing for her sanity would be to get a new phone, now that her number seemed to be out there in the public arena, however that had happened.

'Arapera, this is Liam. I know your life is in turmoil and the weirdoes are hounding you. I can offer you a safe place, where nobody will find you for as long as you like. All modern conveniences and as much solitude as you wish. Just reply and say yes and I'll pick you up. I feel responsible for the way your life has been flicked into the public domain and I want to make amends. No ties, no expectations – just peace and quiet.'

Liam? She only knew one Liam, if you could call it knowing someone you only met while you lay under a crashed car. Or was this a scam, someone from media wanting to trick her into a conversation where she might reveal something new or to get her to discuss her father?

How do I know if my judgement is reliable now, she thought despondently, and stared at the window covered in runnels of rain to match her mood. How do I know if it's him or someone tricking me? And if it is the Liam from the accident, what is he really offering me?

Stumbling out of bed and heading for the shower, she wished that Carter was there so she could discuss this with him, but he would have left at twenty past six as he always did when he was on the early shift.

While she was getting dressed there was a knock on the door and she stood frozen in place for a moment holding her breath, before rational thought returned, and she shook herself. Nobody could get in, so why did she feel so scared? As long as she didn't open the door, she was safe. There was no further knock, so she finished dressing and picked up the phone on her way to the kitchen to make breakfast. But once her toast was on a plate, she didn't want it, she felt repulsed by the thought of chewing and swallowing, so she left the phone and the plate on the bench and lay down on the sofa.

It's pathetic, she thought, this harassment has taken over my mind, and I feel as if I'm having a breakdown, I'm exhausted all the time, and this sofa has become the centre of my universe. I can't imagine how stars cope with abuse and attention and everything about them and their families being discussed and gossiped about by people they've never met. I never realised before how valuable privacy is, the feeling that your home is a safe place where nobody can get to you. Though in my early life my home wasn't safe, of course, but generally that's how it should be. And now my life is taken over by strangers, my phone number and email address seem to be available to everyone, and there is no safe space for me to retreat to, I've turned into a commodity.

She could never have imagined that she would react like this, not the girl who always kept her cool and never flinched, unless in private. The girl who was renowned on the netball circuit for playing to the end of the final quarter of an important game with a broken middle finger that had turned into a swollen red sausage by the time the game was over.

Reluctantly she got up and read the text message

again, because if it was really Liam, she wanted to talk to him. She had wished she could talk to him ever since the day of the accident, but how would she know if this was a scam. And then suddenly she knew what to do and texted back, '*What did you say when I told you my name?*'

Five minutes later a reply arrived, '*I think I said What a pretty name, I haven't met an Arapera before. Maybe not those exact words, but something like it.*'

She thought for a moment and asked another question. '*And what did I say?*'

This time the response was immediate. '*You said it had been the name of your grandmother and great-grandmother, I think, and it skipped your mother's generation.*'

And as opposed to how she would have reacted a week or two ago, it only took her a couple of seconds to decide that she trusted him, that this was an offer of refuge and peace, just what she needed. She thought back to that interminable time she spent under the car and how calmly he talked to her, how he made her feel that the situation was perfectly normal, and all would be well. She picked up her phone again and sent a text, '*Yes please, I would like to get away from here for a couple of days.*'

'*When do you want to be picked up?*'

'*Any time that suits you.*'

'*I'll be outside at half past ten, will text when I arrive. White Volvo, just come out and get in and we'll go, but no rush.*'

'*Where are we going? Do you know where I live?*'

'Yes, I know where you live. We're going to the Mana Marina – it's where I live on my boat Stillwater.'

At twenty to eleven Arapera opened the passenger door of the white Volvo parked outside her block of flats and got in with a small bag. She looked across at the driver but the only thing she recognized were the grey eyes and the tousled brown hair. And who can tell one pair of grey eyes from another pair, she thought, suddenly anxious again. I thought he was older than this – what if it's not him after all? And her hand went instinctively to the doorhandle.

'Hang on,' said the driver and half turned in his seat, tilted his head as close to a ninety-degree angle as he could and smiled. 'Recognize me now?'

'Sorry, I get a bit paranoid at times,' said Arapera, and though she had not recognized his face, she did recognize his voice. 'I know it's you – but these horrible ideas pop up in my head at odd times. Yesterday a talk-show host tried to bully her way into the flat by pretending she was delivering flowers – probably to interview me about my parents! As if ...' She stops, unable to carry on.

'I saw the video – as if having to cope with the actual event wasn't enough. That was very cool that way you got her to step back, very quick. It's getting a lot of admiring attention on social media today.'

'That's what Carter said too, my flatmate. Oh

heavens, see? My mind is scrambled – I must text him and say I've gone away - I haven't told him yet.'

She spent a few minutes composing a long message to Carter, knowing he might not have time to read it until the end of his shift, but she felt better having done it; giving him the details of where she was going and with whom would stop him worrying. And then, suddenly and for no obvious reason she felt exhausted again, leaned her head back and closed her eyes. When she woke up, they were already on the motorway north and the sun was shining. Embarrassed at maybe having been studied while she was unaware, she gripped her hands together tight and stared down at her lap. Liam looked across and smiled, calm as always.

'Feeling better?'

'I think so – I didn't mean to fall asleep. But lately I haven't slept well … and last night was hopeless. That email and meeting her yesterday, it did my head in.'

'Who?'

'Oh sorry, you don't know. An email from the mother of those two girls, the ones who were killed years ago, Caroline Hudson. She asked to meet me, and she wanted to know how they looked and if I saw their faces and …'

Suddenly tears were running down her cheeks and she stopped talking, overwhelmed by her feeling of guilt that she hadn't been able to lie to give Caroline comfort. The memory of Caroline's voice saying that she had seen her children crushed to death right in front of her swamped her, just at it had the previous day and she couldn't continue speaking.

'Never mind telling me now,' said Liam without looking across at her. 'Save it until we're there – and only tell me if you really want to. I'm not expecting anything from you – this is about you, not about me.'

Chapter 27

Despite having driven through Mana many times on her way north, Arapera had never realised that directly north of the bridge, behind the houses and the railway, lay a large marina. Liam drove in, parked facing the quay, turned the motor off and turned to look at her.

'My boat is the first one on the left of the pier just in front of us – she's longer than what they normally allow, and they gave me that berth so I'm not sticking out and making it hard for other boats to get past. And I pay for two berths, so I have no immediate neighbours.'

'What is it? Is it a houseboat – without a house on top?'

'I suppose you could say it's a houseboat, because I live on it - the living quarters are below deck. It was a barge, which is a great thing for living on, because the sides of a barge don't curve in like on most boats and the hull is straight and very wide, so there's loads of room inside. It's just like a modern two-bedroom flat.'

Walking across to the pier, Arapera noticed the name Stillwater painted on the side and had to smile. 'Do you ever take it out to sea or is it just a floating house? Is that why it's called Stillwater?'

'I pick a good, calm day to take her out to sea, but I don't do it very often.' Liam chuckled. 'She rocks and tilts like anything unless it's very calm, not built for the open sea. But it's mainly just where I live – with the occasional little excursion now and then.'

'Amazing!' said Arapera when they went down the steps from the wheelhouse on the deck and she found herself in what looked just like a comfortable, modern apartment, apart from the fact that all the windows were round. 'I had no idea it would be so big inside.'

'My bedroom is at that end, and this is the main cabin – living room and kitchen. The guestroom is over there with the door to the engine room in the corner. The bathroom is the door beside the fridge at my end. Would you like a cup of coffee, or do you need a sleep?'

When she opened her eyes, she felt as if she had slept for hours and she lay without moving, calmer than at any time for the last couple of weeks. Her gaze moved around the room; pale greyish blue walls, dark blue curtains beside the two portholes and three large, famed photos of waves crashing over rocks on the walls. She was covered by a colourful quilt which she couldn't remember pulling over herself. In fact, she could only vaguely remember going into the room and lying down. Through the open door she heard soft sounds, but she felt too indolent to get up and investigate. When she coughed a voice from the main cabin said, 'Are you awake? Time for lunch?'

Standing in the doorway, still sleep-muddled, she said, 'What time is it?' and Liam looked up from his laptop. 'Just after one.'

'Are you …?' She stopped, unable to bring herself to ask.

'No, I'm not writing about you. I'm writing a blog post about the wilding pine problem in the South Island and how it will be a tragedy if the elimination funding is cut. It's been going so well ever since the pandemic, and they created all those environmental jobs.'

'Sorry! I didn't really think you'd write about me today.' She sat down on the curved sofa built into the corner beside the door to the guest room. 'As I said before, I've lost my sense of proportion – everything seems threatening or strange and I react in the wrong way.'

She paused and looked down; the last thing she wanted was to talk about her crazy family, but he already knew and had commented on his website, and she felt she should explain. 'Ever since my father went public with his demonic possession theory, it feels as if everybody in the world has the right to comment on me and my life. But they don't just comment, they want to meet me or take selfies or … all kinds of mad things. I feel as if I'm public property.'

'That's why you're here.' He paused until she looked directly at him. 'I wrote about your amazing resilience under that car because I thought it was epic the way you coped - style and grace and courage - and then my blog post set in motion this monster movement of invasive interest that's ruining your life. And when I found out you had resigned from your job, I decided the only practical thing I could do for you was to offer you sanctuary here.'

'I'm not blaming you! How could you possibly have known what it would develop into? I'm very grateful to be here. My friend Carmen offered me a bed at her place, but everyone who knows her would find out and I still wouldn't feel as if I was away from it all. But this is lovely – like being on another planet.'

Liam got up and stretched. 'To me it is another planet, and I'm lucky to have it. You're welcome to share it for as long as you like. When does your new job start?'

'How do you know about my new job?'

'Someone sent an email and told me. Now that your name is everywhere and my blog has become flavour of the week, people feed me all kinds of snippets. I don't know how he knows, but somehow, he does. Maybe he knows your employer? It was quite funny, because I don't think he realises that he's met me a couple of times with friends. This happens now and then - someone I actually know comments or emails me and doesn't realise it's me, they take for granted they're writing to a stranger, because they don't know it's me writing the blog. This guy said it's some kind of IT job for a private company.'

'Yes, but only partly that – part of the time I'll be a kind of trusted confidant handling valuable items and dispatching them to buyers all over the world.'

She smiled, and suddenly she felt normal again, as if a switch had been flicked, truly normal and not frazzled by her parents or concerned at all the attention her family was getting subjected to. The transformation was as wonderful as it was unexpected. It must be the environment, she thought, the silence and the calm and the way he's so honest and straight. I must be very careful not to take advantage, not to play the poor little me game and make him feel trapped into looking out for me long term.

'The job was offered to me after I had a row with my manager – who's a total twit who can't make up his mind about anything in less than three days.'

She smiled at the memory of that fateful meeting with Shane and Fiona. 'And he complained about me to the CEO, who's a very pompous man, and he gave me a formal warning. The damn toad! He also put me on three-monthly performance reviews, so I resigned. That new job was an unexpected gift from the gods.'

Liam chuckled and she recognised the way his eyes crinkled even though his head wasn't at a ninety-degree angle. 'I bet you did it very effectively – the resignation, I mean. And how come this change of mood? What snapped you out of your misery? I've been seriously worried about you up to one minute ago - and now you seem to be back to what I assume is more like your normal self.'

'I don't know – it might be how safe I feel here or …'

He ignored the way her voice died away, as if he could sense her feeling that she had nearly said something unacceptable, something she might regret. She could not possible have nearly said "because of you", could she? She shivered at the thought of complicating this strange and very new friendship, which she already sensed might prove vital to her mental wellbeing. She knew nothing about him, and she must keep it neutral and unemotional.

'Let's have lunch,' said Liam, changing the topic and the mood with one short sentence and turned towards the kitchen bench. 'Scrambled eggs?'

Arapera didn't even realise she had fallen asleep again leaning against the big cushions on the sofa with her Kindle in her hand after lunch. She surfaced slowly and lay still trying once again to work out how she came to be lying on the curved sofa, once again covered with a rug, without recalling how it had happened. Liam was not in sight, but she heard him talking to someone and realised he was up on the deck above her head. She saw his shadow moving across the large skylight in the ceiling and then something small ran across the glass very fast, and she remembered that he had mentioned a cat in one of his blog posts.

Standing at the top of the stairs that ended in the little wheelhouse on deck, she looked around and took in the scene that she had only half registered when they arrived. The Stillwater lay alongside a finger of a main pier with an empty space between her and the wharf and seemed a lot bigger than the other boats, and very different in shape. She could see now that it was nearly rectangular, not with the pronounced curve in the hull you see on most boasts, with the wheelhouse nearly in the middle and large deck areas at both ends.

It's lovely, she thought, like having an apartment on the top floor of a building and a roof terrace with room for chairs and a table and a barbecue and lots more. I never thought it could be like this. But how does it work? Toilets, power, water, rubbish − there must be systems that you pay for if you live here, and they must have fuel for the boats too. It's like a different world and I never thought of it before. And then a cat appeared beside her feet, a little black cat with a white chest and white paws.

'Meet Essie,' said Liam coming around the corner of the wheelhouse. 'Named after my older sister Esmeralda, who lives in Hungary, she's a violinist. This is my second Essie, well third if you start with my sister.'

'I need to tell a few people where I am − those I can trust.' Leaning back on the sofa that evening she looked up at the skylight which now looked like a grey rectangle. 'And I want to talk to Carter - I texted him this morning from the car, and he's replied, but I need to talk to him.'

'Your parents? And your brother?'

'No, not my father, of course, but I'll tell my brother Jackson, he'll keep it to himself,' she said slowly, a frown crease between her eyebrows as she considered this. 'I think I'll say I'm out of town to for a while with a friend without explaining who or where. If I tell him I resigned and my new job does start for a few weeks, he won't ask any questions. He's not very curious about things. And at the moment he is so furious with my father that he'll probably not talk to him for ages.'

'What will you do if your father calls?'

'I've blocked his number − I can't face talking to him just now.' She could hear her voice getting louder and knew the strain of even thinking about a conversation with either of her parents was kicking in.

'Don't think about it,' he said calmly and reached for the bottle of wine on the little table between them. 'If it makes you stressed talking about it, just send the text to your brother and leave it at that.'

She reached over to take the glass he was holding out towards her. 'You're right − I won't tell anyone apart from Carter that I'm with you − they'd all get the wrong idea. Carter won't − we always understand each other. I'll send a group message to my friends that I'm normally in touch with and say I'm going away for a while before I start my new job. And by the way, how did you know where I live?'

'I shouldn't have let you know that I'd found out your address,' he said, his eyes on her face in a way that made her feel that whatever her initial reaction was, he didn't want to miss it. 'I hope you won't feel I've stalked you, but I felt so responsible for the mess your private life had become, and I tried to think of all the worst things those nutters – the ones who're into ghosts and whatever – what they might take it into their heads to do.'

The corner of his mouth twitched when she shook her head. 'Yeah, I know – some ghosts obviously do exist for certain people at certain times, but you know what I mean. People whose whole lives revolve around mystical things, the more unprovable the better. At one stage what was being said on social media was extreme and quite scary, and I began to worry about your safety. And here's the confession - I parked outside your place a couple of days, just sat in the car and watched to see what would happen at the times you went out or came home. Checking if anyone hung around your block of flats, who went in and out.'

And then he chuckled, and Arapera smiled because his chuckle was so infectious. 'That tall guy in hospital scrubs, blond, Viking-looking giant – that must be Carter? Yeah, I thought so. Are you related?'

She looked quizzically at him with her head tilted to one side. 'I can see why you ask – we're so alike it would be easy to think we're brother and sister.' She reached behind her and lifted a handful of nearly black tresses while pointing at her brown eyes with the forefinger of the other hand. '*Such* a family likeness, we could be twins – people often remark on it.'

That made him laugh, which made her feel good and nearly normal; to make a silly joke and hear someone laugh made up for a lot of stress.

'But no, we've been great friends since high school when he was worried about coming out as gay because of how his family would react, particularly his grandfather. So, we made a deal – I would pretend to be his girlfriend, and if he decided to come out, or when he did, then we'd have a pretend splitting-up and just be friends.'

Telling him about Carter and the various boyfriend/girlfriend scenes they had enacted, and how they showed off their romantic dancing skills at the senior ball, took ten minutes. Making Liam laugh made her feel happy and proud, as if she had achieved something special, and every time he laughed as some ridiculous part of the story, she had to smile too.

'And he's a bit older than you?'

'He's twenty-nine, two years older. He's my best friend.' She looked up at the skylight for a moment and smiled at the sight of Essie lying on it looking like roadkill with her fur flattened against the glass.

'He moved in with me when I had to get a mortgage on the flat.'

'After that bastard took half?'

Suddenly it struck her that they hadn't talked about this, and she felt devastated that she had not even acknowledged what he achieved, not thanked him.

'Oh God, I'm sorry - I should have said! What you

did about that was amazing and I'm so grateful – the whole thing was a nightmare. He left me – after the three required years, of course, and I thought it was just a divorce and cursed the fact I had fallen for someone so shallow and egocentric.' She shook her head at the memory of how she had been taken in. 'He was a lot older – and very good looking, and kind of charismatic, very convincing. I fell for it – and now, looking back, I'm sure it was planned, a deliberate strategy. You see, early on I realised he knew I owned the apartment, I didn't just rent it – something he said revealed that and it wasn't until much later the significance of that became clear. And then he took half my assets as you say, and I had no idea it was a scam until you put it in your blog. But he would have been able to even if he hadn't married me – according to the law, I mean.'

'Did you see how it came to light? That chain of coincidence that culminated with the guy in Tasmania tagging his sister, Wendy? And the crazy woman I went out with, the one who wanted ten thousand dollars? And as I said in a recent post, I don't think he's legally entitled to half your assets – not after committing a crime by marrying you. Personally, I think he didn't know that cohabiting equated to being married.'

Getting up with his empty glass in his hand he stopped beside her and reached for hers. And suddenly she realised that this man, still very much an unknown quantity, who came into her life in such a strange way, had not only rescued her from sliding into depression, but he was more now than an impromptu friend. On an impulse she reached out and grasped his free hand and looked up at his face. 'You have done so much for me - I don't know how to thank you.'

His fingers curled around hers for a moment and she could see the precise moment when he held back from saying what he had been just about to say, when his eyes flicked away for a fraction of a second. What had he been about to tell her? Suddenly she just had to know, and she said, 'Yes?'

But the moment was gone. 'Good,' was all he said before letting go of her hand and taking their glasses to the kitchen bench.

Returning to sit at the end of the sofa he asked, sounding slightly hesitant, 'How were you able to afford an apartment at that age? If you don't mind telling me? It seems from what I know now that you owned it outright with no mortgage, which is very unusual for someone so young.'

'I won Lotto – enough to buy the flat and nearly enough left of to furnish it. I met my fake husband only a couple of months later. Thank God for Carter! He had ditched his partner just at the time when I had to get a mortgage, so I could pay my so-called husband after the divorce – I had to have a flatmate. I wasn't quite in the income bracket to cope without someone paying rent and there's nobody in the world I'd rather share my flat with than Carter.'

Two days later, when the breakfast dishes were tidied away, Liam asked, 'What do you need? Any shopping, more stuff from the flat? I noticed you only brought a very small bag. We can walk from here to the shops or take the car and drive into Wellington – just say what you want to do.'

'If you give me directions, I'll go for a walk this morning.'

'I'll come with you.'

'Oh, there's no need – just point me in the right direction. I don't want to take up your time.' The last thing she wanted was to become a tiresome burden, someone who had to be looked after like an invalid.

Liam looked at her with a slight smile, but she sensed serious intent behind it. 'Sorry, but that's just how it is, it's not negotiable. I'm not going to risk someone spotting you and making a nuisance of themselves taking selfies – or trying to give you bunches of flowers. And a walk is always nice anyway.'

There was something behind that smile, some other concern that she didn't understand. Studying him as he sat at the far end of the sofa with his feet up and his eyes now back on the book that rested on his bent knees, she briefly contemplated asking him why. Why did he feel he had to go with her? Definitely not just that people might want to take selfies, the idea was ridiculous, but she said nothing.

Being onboard Stillwater was like being in a cocoon of calm, and even the thought of some undefined future publicity didn't have the power to make her feel unsettled. Wait and see, she thought and let her gaze slide away from his face. Maybe it's just that he feels responsible now that I'm his guest. If it's anything worse, I'll find out in due course.

Over the last couple of days, she had begun to decipher his face, learnt to read the tiny signals of mood or intention. The way the left corner of his mouth turned up ever so slightly when he was teasing or secretly amused, the way two perfectly parallel creases appeared between his eyebrows when he was thinking about what he was writing, sitting perfectly still and gazing into the middle distance as if he had to find exactly the right word or phrase to make every sentence perfect.

'You're very good at writing,' she said abruptly, following up her thoughts with a voiced comment that surprised her as much as it did him. 'I mean, your blog – I love the way you write. It looks simple and very casual, but it's concise and somehow feels personal. I imagine it conveys exactly what you intend, no more and no less, and it leaves no room for misunderstanding your intentions – such a talent.'

His face was unreadable for all of two seconds, and then she saw the left corner of his mouth tweak up and he said, 'Now, where did that come from, all of a sudden? But thank you, I'm glad you like my writing. It was something I started enjoying when I was with the army – helicopter pilots spend quite a lot of time waiting – for action, to be needed, for others to be ready, for loads to be secured onboard. Plenty of time to write down observations, little snapshots of what goes on around you, if you carry a notebook.'

'This isn't what I call a real walk,' said Arapera when they reached the Mana shops. 'This was just a short stroll. I had no idea it was so close.'

'Very handy,' said Liam and grasped her wrist. 'No, don't take the cap off. I know I said I'm mainly concerned about those who live on their boats in the marina – they've never seen a woman on my boat before, not apart from my teenage cousin, so they'd have a damn good look. But some of them might be in the supermarket and they'll stop and talk. I'm going to introduce you as my girlfriend from Auckland. What's your favourite name apart from your own?'

'I don't think I have one but tell people I'm called Ara if you need to introduce me – like a short form of Arapera and then you won't slip up if you start saying the wrong thing. I actually had a very good friend called Ara when I was a student, short for some very long Indian name – he lives in Melbourne now.'

'Now,' said Liam and stopped at the pedestrian crossing. 'I'll show you where the laundromat is – I use it if the one at the marina is busy and I'm in a hurry. This thing about not being allowed to hang washing on the boats is a bit of a nuisance at times. The driers take longer than the washing machines, so sometimes it turns into a long wait for a drier. Never mind, I've changed my mind about crossing here - let's walk down this side of the street and then cross and come back on the other side later.'

'And why is that?' She was getting good at decoding him now, and she knew for a fact there was something behind this decision. 'You're not the kind of man who makes a decision without a good reason.'

'The café, the one down there.' He laughed. 'It's the one I like best, and I had the devious thought that we could have morning coffee and a brownie before we have bags of shopping to carry.'

Within minutes Liam's earlier prediction was

proved right. They had no sooner entered the café than a loud voice called out. 'Liam! Over here – come and join us.'

'I don't think we have a choice,' said Liam quietly out of the corner of his mouth. 'He's four boats up from me and not a man to be denied.' He raised his hand in greeting and called back, 'Hi, Sinbad! We'll just order first.'

'Sinbad – really?' Arapera tried unsuccessfully not to laugh as they moved towards the counter.

'Look over towards the window,' said Liam. 'Just a quick glance around – and then tell me if you can work out who in here would be called Sinbad.'

Arapera let her gaze sweep slowly around the café without pausing on the man with the white beard and a peaked captain's hat. 'Aha - of course, he's called Sinbad. What's his wife called – Scheherazade?'

'Margaret,' said Liam and the corner of his mouth tweaked up. 'Such a let-down, sorry.'

They made their way to Sinbad's table and the closer they got, the more obvious became the intense scrutiny Arapera was being subjected to.

'And who have we got here?' boomed Sinbad before Liam had a chance to introduce her. 'This is one for the books, eh? Didn't think you approved of women on boats.'

'Ara,' said Liam calmly, 'meet my friends Sinbad and Margaret. They're on that nice yacht with the dark blue hull I pointed out yesterday – four berths up from us.'

'Lovely to meet you,' said Arapera and sat down beside Margaret on the principle that the further she sat from Sinbad the less likely was it that her hearing would be damaged. She soon discovered the downside, however, because now Sinbad could stare at her without even turning his head, a scrutiny that seemed excessive, but she continued without pause, 'I've only been here for a couple of days, but I love it – such a lovely change from the Auckland traffic fumes. I'd only been here at night before and seeing this part of the coast in daylight is a real treat.'

She gave Liam a glowing smile, and he smiled back. 'It's about time you came down for a proper holiday – Auckland isn't my favourite place, as you know.'

Margaret, who had been giving Arapera a thorough once-over, leaned in close. 'How long have you two known each other?'

'Oh, must be about six months, I think,' said Arapera and Liam said, 'Longer, more like eight. And how are you two – I haven't seen you for a few days.'

'Bloody appointments.' Sinbad scowled. 'We're getting decrepit – there's forever something or other wrong with one of us. Lately we've had to go into town nearly every week.'

'It's not that bad, just a few niggles.' Margaret sounded as if she was well used to de-escalating Sinbad's outbursts. 'Sinbad's got a wonky hip that keeps him awake at night, so he had to have an x-ray.'

'Enough about my hip!' Sinbad was not the kind of man who wanted his masculinity diminished by discussing details of his health issues. 'You're a dark dog, Liam! I've never known you to have a woman on your boat since we've been here.'

Liam cast a fond look at Arapera and said, 'Only this special girl – I never found anyone interesting enough before.'

By the time they left the café, Arapera was glad to escape. 'God, that was quite intensive!' she said when they were out of earshot. 'I hope it worked.'

'I think we were perfect, born actors - they totally believed every word we said. And that bit about what you do for a job – hilarious. I nearly laughed out loud.'

She grinned. 'You have to give them some leeway, Liam – a lot of people their age probably don't know what a programmer does.'

'When she asked if you worked for RNZ it took me a moment to figure out where she was coming from, but your explanation was so kind – I know they're overly inquisitive, but we don't want to make them feel silly.'

'Of course. we don't. I think it went really well. And now we've established that you've got a woman friend, who's been onboard only at *night* before – I thought that was brilliant, even if I say so myself. Gave them something to use their imaginations on. Like I came swooping down from Auckland and only stayed the night and then left at dawn.'

'Ah yes, I'm sure they are picturing a night of unbridled passion. Margaret will spread the word. There aren't that many who live permanently on their boats, so they tend to act as if we're all part of a little community, but it can get a bit much at times.'

Chapter 30

Her voice a mixture of apprehension and disgust, Arapera said, 'Oh God, what's happened now? Carmen just sent a text with a warning but no link to where she saw this — it's going to fuel all kinds of horrible stuff again.'

The way Liam looked up from his laptop and considered her face before he replied told her he knew what she was talking about. 'I've seen it — do you want me to summarize, or do you want to read it for yourself?'

After thinking for only a moment she picked up her laptop that now lived permanently on the coffee table just next to where she always sat in the corner of the sofa. 'Just tell me where to find it and I'll read it myself.'

'Search for "demon in pink bag" — it's all over the place.'

She met his eyes briefly before he looked down at

his keyboard again and apprehension formed a hard lump in her chest. A few minutes later she looked up from her laptop, flushed with an uncomfortable mix of fury and embarrassment.

'Dan!' she exclaimed. 'That cheap bastard – he's the only one who knows that ending, because that's *not* how it ended and …'

Liam's was looking across the room in a considering way as if he was trying to decide if he should get up or stay where he was, as if some kind of intervention might be needed.

Arapera tried to sound normal, but as soon as she opened her mouth, she knew she had failed. 'I lied to him, because I couldn't bear to tell him how it really ended, so I left out the worst part and invented a less traumatic ending.' She stopped to draw breath, suddenly back in that awful place in her mind where she had no privacy and no rights. Where people could gossip about her in a public forum, spread rumours and make any kind of comments they liked.

'There was something worse than what's in that article?' Liam sounded incredulous and she knew that she should probably tell him but talking about it made her feel sick. Images appeared in her mind, random fragments of humiliating memories and scenes of painful punishments, rapidly displacing each other, an assault on her composure that tormented her. In the blink of an eye, her mind had her back on the kitchen floor with a large and menacing man leaning over her, knowing there was no help coming, and whatever he was going to do, he would do.

She leaned her head back against the sofa and closed her eyes and felt a tear roll down her cheek. 'Oh yes,' she said without opening her eyes, 'I didn't tell him the half of it - what really happened was much, much worse and I can't ...'

This was the most awful thing that could have happened, the worst episode of her strange home life becoming public knowledge. She felt another tear sliding down her cheek and made no move to wipe it away. Staying very still without opening her eyes was like hiding her pain, not seeing pity on Liam's face. She heard his footsteps on the wooden floor, and leapt to her feet, her only thought to get to her bedroom and close the door and regain control, not have him witness her distress,.

'Come here,' he said and pulled her towards him, his arms holding her tight with one hand on her back and the other holding her head against his shoulder. 'Don't cry - we'll sort this out together. I'll help you take the heat out of this.'

They stood there for a long time without speaking or moving, and in Arapera's mind logic and composure slid slowly back into place, the feeling of apprehension that had nearly overwhelmed her receded, and her body relaxed against his.

Still with her face against his shoulder she said in a

muffled voice, 'Yes, please,' but she made no move to take a step back, and Liam continued to hold her.

'Who is Dan?' he asked instead of replying, and she knew she must tell him the whole story, however awful it would make her feel.

'He's a guy I dated for about six months, but he did something totally heinous, so I ditched him about a month ago.'

Her voice gave her away, she could hear it herself; the loathing she felt for Dan after what he did to her.

'What did he do?' This time Liam wasn't asking with an unspoken "if you don't mind telling me", he sounded determined and nearly angry.

He needs to know, thought Arapera, perhaps then he'll understand that I'm not weak and needing help, that I've actually had some dreadful things happen to me lately, and they've all added up to how vulnerable I feel at the moment. I want him to know that aside from recently, I have spent my life from the age of five being staunch and not letting things drag me down, not even violence or terror.

'I found out he'd sent a text to another woman about me – or rather about how much more exciting she was in bed compared to me, quite detailed.' She raised her head and looked straight into his eyes and took control of her voice, speaking calmly and without emphasis. 'It was pure chance I got to hear about it. The woman he sent it to, showed it to someone else, who told her friend. You know how it goes – too interesting a piece of gossip to keep to yourself. And that friend, she knows me, we were at uni together – we both belonged to the fencing club. She was outraged to find that not only was he playing away, but his message was being shared all over town, so she told me. I'd thought he was nice enough - you know, I wasn't in love with him, or not very much, but he was good company and funny, and it was nice to go out with someone who actually reads books.'

'I read books,' said Liam and leant his head against hers, and she surprised herself by the little gurgle of amusement that caught in her throat. 'Of course, you do. You read *and* write – you're old school.'

He held her away from him with his hands on her upper arms and said, 'Too old?'

She had no idea what he was really asking. There was no clue to what had prompted his question, and his face revealed nothing. 'Oh God, no – you're not *old*, you just have that kind of older era inclination, from the days when people actually cared about how they phrased things and punctuated properly. How old are you?'

'Eleven years, three months and … ah, four days older than you.'

She saw the little twitch at the corner of his mouth and realised that he was laughing at himself, because he had just admitted that he knew practically everything about her. Not just her address and phone number, her crazy family history and her disastrous marriage, but her exact age too.

'Can we please have a cup of coffee now - and talk about how to defuse this damn article?'

'You make it this time, it's time you earned your keep,' he said with pretend severity and dropped his hands. 'You've been mollycoddled long enough, and you're bouncing back faster every time you've nearly crumpled. I'm sure you've noticed where everything's kept. I'm going to the bathroom.'

When they had their mugs of coffee, Arapera said, 'So, I was a research subject? You set about finding out everything about me?'

'Yes, I did set out to find out all I could when I realised what I had unleashed - the damage I had inflicted on you. Not that I meant to, but I'm still responsible.'

She said nothing, just kept her gaze on his face until he continued. 'I felt responsible even at the time of the accident, but in a different way. I stayed and listened to you negotiating about the bandage with the ambulance guy until he gave in, and until you limped away - in case you needed help.'

'Why did you hang around all that time? You stayed there after the emergency services had arrived and you never even took a step away – I could see your feet when you got up so the rescue service guy could talk to me, you were right there the whole time. Even when they'd propped up the car and I was safe you lay down on the ground again.'

He shrugged. 'Yeah, I knew you were supposedly safe then – but what if the car had fallen even after they propped it up? The damn thing creaked and groaned every time the people inside it moved even a tiny bit. You would have been crushed. I felt you were nearly at the same level of risk you'd been in from the start, just that with the props in place the car would have fallen from a slightly higher starting point - and I had a plan.'

'A plan?'

'A very primitive plan.' He gave her a wry look. 'If the car fell, if the front started slipping off that ledge, I'd push in under it - as soon as I heard the first graunch of metal on concrete. I was prepared, ready to go.'

For a moment she could only stare at him in amazement, and then she said slowly, 'You're completely mad – you would have been crushed too!'

'Yes, but at least you would have had someone beside you. And maybe my body would have held the car a bit further off the ground – and off you. I reckoned my head and my ribcage are bigger than yours and much stronger.' He smiled at her expression of outrage. 'It's not as crazy as it sounds. I knew I wouldn't have a chance to get my whole body in under the car, but I thought I had a good chance of pushing half of me in.' He paused briefly. 'I kind of felt that having been the first to spot you under that car and the way we seemed to …'

'What? What did we seem to do?'

His gaze slid away. 'I can't explain – or at least not without making an idiot of myself. Let it lie.'

'I did too.' Her voice was as steady.

'What did you do too?'

'The same thing - I felt the connection. As if we'd been through something together and come out the other end. Survived some kind of test of hardship and danger without losing our cool and without drama - and because we did it together, we're linked.'

She had never felt so serious in her life, so intent on making someone else understand exactly what she meant. This was something she had held close to her heart since the accident; the connection that had existed only in her mind before she said it out loud, but she knew that he had felt it too.

They looked at each other for a long moment, then she said, 'Now, will you tell me honestly what it is you know that you haven't told me yet? You made me wear a cap with my hair tucket up when we walked to the village – and sunglasses – and it wasn't just because you never had a woman on the boat before and people would be curious, was it? Someone's told you something and you're determined that nobody's going to be able to find me even here. This isn't just about respite, it's like a safe house.'

He made no reply, just looked out the porthole again with the frown creases back between his eyebrows.

'I can sense it, Liam. Not that your other reasons are lies, they're probably true too, but there's something worse hiding behind those reasons and if it concerns me, I need to know what it is.'

'OK – I'll tell you. I wasn't going to yet in case it made it harder for you.' He was looking at her as if he was evaluating the wisdom of telling her, as if he hoped she would cope. 'I know you're incredibly strong and composed normally, but this isn't a normal situation we're in at the moment, and you're already under pressure. There's a couple, at the moment somewhere in Taranaki, I think, and they've made some quite irrational and serious threats against you. A guy who follows my blog contacted me via my website and told me about it and gave me some links to these people's social media accounts.'

'And?' In Arapera's mind questions formed so rapidly that she didn't know what to ask first. 'Tell me, please.'

'Well, I told the cops about what I've managed to find out so far, and they're trying to locate this couple and give them a warning. Something along lines of not issuing threats of serious harm against another person. But if they're truly crazy – which seems likely to me – then a warning from the police probably isn't going to be very effective. That's why I decided I needed to get you out of harm's way.'

She sat silent for a long time, absent-mindedly looking at her bare feet and he watched her without moving. Finally, she looked up and gave him a wry smile.

'About the interview Dan did - I'll call Carter and let you talk to him. Just so you can honestly say someone other than me told you the whole story, including the real ending. And then you can write about it – because that's what you meant, isn't it? When you said you know how to deal with it - you mean to somehow take Dan on?'

'Yes, I'd like to name and shame him if you don't mind, but I'd like to meet Carter in person rather than talk to him on the phone. We can drive into town and go to your apartment, or he can come here – whatever you prefer. And I suppose you'd like to pick up some more clothes perhaps?'

'I'll text him and ask him to come here, but when depends on his roster at the hospital. I think I'd rather see him here than go into town. He's got my car and the keys so he can get here easily. I'll tell you about the pink bag when Carter's here if you don't mind. It's a bit difficult ...'

Chapter 32

Carter arrived two days later, on a perfect day with sunshine glittering on the water and hardly any breeze. 'Where did you park?' asked Liam. 'You could have driven in and parked in the visitors' space.'

'I took the train. I haven't been on a train for years, not since I was a little kid, and our class went on a ride somewhere and back. I can't even remember where we went. But it's great – you get to see the landscape and the coast from a completely different angle, and you can really look, not just glance to one side like when you're driving.'

Liam nodded. 'I nearly always take the train when I go into town. Let's face it, it's not that you need to walk very far to get everywhere in Wellington, and you avoid a lot of hassle. Let's have lunch up here on the deck seeing it's a nice day.'

Still with his arm over Arapera's shoulders, where

he had stood since he first came onboard, Carter gave her a squeeze. 'You look a lot better than you did last time I saw you – I'm really pleased. I was worried sick about you, girl, couldn't stop thinking of how you'd cope if your dad turned up and banged on the door when I was at work.'

He let her go and turned to Liam. 'Nice boat! Must have been one of those huge barges they had decades ago to unload cargo – did you convert it yourself?'

'Why don't you two get to know each other and I'll prepare lunch,' said Arapera before Liam had a chance to reply. 'I'll hand up a couple of beers in a moment.'

She suddenly felt that she wanted to avoid having a discussion about her problematic life straight away, that somehow it would feel more comfortable if this started out as a normal social situation. Without waiting for an answer, she ran down the stairs to the cabin and returned a moment later with two bottles.

'Here you are,' she said and went back down, but remained at the foot of the stairs for a moment listening as Liam started telling Carter about the boat before she turned to the fridge and began slowly getting things out for lunch.

I'll give them at least ten minutes, she thought, or as much time as I can until Liam starts wondering what I'm doing. The longer they have to become comfortable with each other, the better. I really want Liam to understand how important my relationship with Carter is, and how much we mean to each other, and to realise for himself that Carter can be trusted. I'm only now beginning to understand how protective Liam is, like a bodyguard – against both physical and mental harm, very like Carter in that respect, and they've got to trust each other.

When she decided she couldn't possibly delay lunch any longer and had given them enough time, she called up the steps to the wheelhouse. 'Liam, this tray is very full and heavy - could you come and take it, please and I'll bring the rest separately?'

By the time the clouds came scudding in from the west and the temperature dropped, they had sat around the table under the big blue umbrella for three hours. They took a load each and retreated inside, where Liam gave Carter a tour that included the engine room, which Arapera remembered had been mentioned on her first day onboard.

'Ha! Special treats for boys?' she said, and Carter looked at Liam with a sly grin. 'You probably haven't had time to discover one of her most useful skills yet. She's very handy with power tools and fixing the blocked drain under the sink and whatever goes wrong. I don't do stuff like that, but I'm always on hand to clean her grazed knuckles and put sticking plaster on her cuts. She's been like it since she was at high school. What was that weird thing I had to buy at Mitre 10 the other day when you installed the peephole in the door?'

'A brad-point drill bit,' she said and laughed inside at the fleeting look of surprise on Liam's face. 'Half inch – just a thing for drilling a big hole that wasn't quite big enough to need a biscuit cutter.'

'Amazing girl! Where did you learn all this?'

'I did wood and metal work at school in Year 10, and then the next couple of years the teacher let me come back after school now and then with another couple of keen kids and learn a bit more. You know - when he was in the workshop anyway. It's been quite useful.'

'I'll say! Very useful for me.' Carter laughed. 'Now, let's check that bag – I couldn't make up my mind about the jeans, but I think I found the right ones, and I put in your running gear including the shoes just in case. There's probably lots of lovely tracks to run on here.'

'So, where to from here?' asked Liam over coffee and biscuits after the tour. 'Arapera has given me permission to name and shame Dan – which will be a pleasure. And I don't mean just in my blog but on all my social media accounts as well, full frontal assault.'

'I had a look at those when I saw the links on your website,' said Carter and picked up another biscuit. 'I found your blog by following a link someone posted on Facebook. What's with the name – I mean on the blog and social media. I presume it's the same everywhere?'

'Yes, Soldierpilotpilot everywhere with my name carefully hidden behind security and privacy settings.'

'What does it mean? I've been wondering ever since I discovered the blog. Were you first a soldier and then a pilot – twice?'

'I know it sounds mad,' said Liam, 'but it's very simple. First, I was a soldier and then they trained me to fly helicopters, so then I was a pilot, and then I left the army and got my commercial pilot's licence for small passenger aircraft, so I became another kind of pilot.'

'OK, very clever name,' said Carter and turned to Arapera. 'But now we must discuss tactics, and I have an idea. You know how you said at lunch that you would really like to go to your mum's engagement party, but you felt a bit nervous. Why are you nervous? Do you think your dad might try to get there?'

'God no! But Jackson said in a text yesterday that Dad had called and asked him if he was going, so he knows about it.'

Her voice trailed off into silence and she sat looking down at the mug in her hand for a moment. 'Perhaps it's just that I don't like him to know what I'm doing, or where I'm likely to be. It sounds a bit ridiculous but it's there in the back of my mind all the time, how lucky it is he doesn't know where I am now, and he doesn't know about my new job.' She smiled at their concerned faces. 'It just makes me feel safer if he knows nothing at all.'

'Why don't we'll all go?' said Liam calmly. 'If you can get the time off, Carter – let's all go together. I'd think having you on one side and me on the other would be enough to keep her safe, we're capable of stopping him from coming too close. If we promise not to leave you alone for even one minute, Arapera?'

'Would you do that? Really? It's a lot to ask, we'd have to either fly to Blenheim or take a car on the ferry.'

'Of course,' said Liam and looked at Carter for confirmation. 'Why wouldn't we? Simple enough. And if Jackson can get a couple of days leave, he can join us. We fly over and hire a car at the other end and go to this vineyard, wherever it is - and book into a motel somewhere handy. Not a problem.'

'But now, poppet, we have to do the hard thing,' said Carter. 'You told me you want to explain the whole exorcism debacle to Liam and that I have to be here for that, so let's not delay it any longer – you've been dreading it, I know, and I'm not surprised. And I think it's important that Liam hears it directly from you, exactly as it happened. And I'll tell him the real ending, the one Dan didn't know, as you said in your message. We'll just listen, and maybe Liam will ask a couple of questions, and you might cry, but that's OK.'

They stayed where they were, Carter and Arapera on the sofa and Liam in the armchair on the other side of the coffee table. She started talking, unable to make eye contact with either of the men, looking down at her hands.

'He never liked me,' she said quietly, 'and I didn't like him, because he punished me a lot, whipped me with the cord from the electric jug if I answered back, right from when I was a little girl – five or six. And then my auntie Jean, who is dad's sister, gave me a pink shoulder bag for my thirteenth birthday and my dad said I was getting worse, and I was arguing too much about religion, and it was because I was possessed by a demon – and the demon must have come with the pink bag.'

She shook her head and hesitated only for a moment, then launched straight into the story, fully aware that if she paused too long, she might never get started. 'So, that morning he forced me to get down on the kitchen floor and he held me down and he put weights on me, big square concrete pavers from the back garden. He had them all ready because I'd said the day before that I wouldn't let him do this exorcism thing, and I wouldn't prostrate myself before God as he called it. And he was furious that I'd argued with him – the day before, I mean - and that I'd managed to run off and stayed out until way after dark. I sneaked in late and slept on the sofa because I didn't dare go upstairs in case he heard me. So, this next day I was hoping he would have calmed down, and I'd be able to go to school, but he'd come down extra early and he was sitting in the kitchen waiting.'

She hesitated and glanced at Carter, who nodded encouragement and after a pause she continued, still not looking directly at either of them, as if not seeing their expressions would make it easier to tell the story.

'Jackson was at a school camp for three days and I think dad had picked that day to punish me because he never beat Jackson, and he probably didn't want him to see what he was going to do. I had to take all my clothes off first of all. I didn't want to, but he started tearing them off me and I said I'd take them off myself, because I didn't want his hands on me. Then he told me to lie on the kitchen floor and he put those pavers on my legs and on each arm, so I was lying as if I was crucified.'

She stopped and cleared her throat. The next part was the worst, worse by far than the beating at the end, because it had made her feel so awful lying there naked, completely at the mercy of a furious, adult man.

'He prayed and prayed, and he shouted at God to give him "the power of the finger of God" so he could expel the demon. He said I would promise to destroy the bag myself and that I would do penance after the demon had left to show how ashamed I was, and I would promise to be a better Christian. And then he went all funny, his face went bright red, and he looked as if he was choking, and it went on and on and then he suddenly roared – like an animal. And I didn't know what he would do next.'

Another long pause while she tried to calm herself and she caught a glance exchanged by the men. She looked at Carter who nodded, and she continued. 'He got the pavers off my arms and legs. He didn't lift them, just pushed them off with his feet – they left wide red grazes on my skin - and then he told me roll over and lie on my front. He had the outside hose coming in through the window above the sink, and he turned the nozzle on and hosed me with cold water, freezing cold, and I wasn't allowed to move. I don't know how long it went on for, but it seemed like a long time - I was shivering with cold, the kitchen was flooded. And then he stopped hosing me and he got a long stick of some kind. I couldn't see what it was, but it was hard, and it didn't bend, and he beat me so hard it broke, and he continued beating me, all up the back of my legs and up to my neck nearly - and the broken end of the stick cut my skin. And then he stopped and he …'

Suddenly it was too much and unable to continue, she looked down at her hands, locked in silene. Carter moved closer and put his arm around her.

'And then,' he said, 'this abominable, cruel man poured salt over her back and walked away saying that if she got up before dusk he would have to start over. She had to stay just where she was, face down, wet and cold with salt in her wounds for the rest of the day.'

'Christ!' said Liam in a voice so unlike his normal voice it was as if a stranger had joined them. 'I'll kill the bastard!'

'I'd join you,' said Carter, 'and it would be a pleasure, but it won't do Arapera any good - she doesn't need any more media attention than she's had already. And by the way, Jackson only found out about the exorcism just recently, so he's still processing it. When you meet him, be careful what you say – he was shattered.'

He tightened his arm around Arapera. 'Don't worry, poppet, I'll tell him the last bit too – you've had enough, and you'll never have to tell anyone again, I promise. So, here's what happened last – Arapera's mother came down from upstairs where she must have heard all this, and she looked at her daughter lying there, naked and beaten and wet – she looked her in the eye and turned around and went back upstairs.'

He tilted Arapera sideways onto the big cushions in the corner of the sofa, handed her a handkerchief, and kept his hand on her hip while Liam got up and returned with a bottle of wine and three glasses.

'That man's a bloody menace - very dangerous. I'm glad you're taking precautions at the flat.' He pushed two glasses across the table and sat down again. 'But why didn't Jackson know until recently?'

Arapera sat up, wiped her eyes and blew her nose, then pushed her hair back over her shoulders. She couldn't quite muster a smile, but she hoped she looked reasonably calm now that the telling was over, and peace was returning to her exhausted mind. This was only the fourth time she had told anyone about the exorcism and each time it left her feeling as if she had lived the events of that day all over again.

'Jackson got on well with dad, right from the start. He's three years younger than I am and dad never did those rants at him, not for anything that I can remember, never beat him. I always thought it must be that I was a girl that made him dislike me – he'd often go on about how Eve ruined the world by listening to the devil and eating that damn apple, as if it was my fault, as if I had done it.'

'What did Jackson think when he found out?' asked Liam gently. 'Had he never asked himself why you got beaten and he was never abused in any way?'

'I don't know what he thought – we've never talked about it, but he knew about everything that dad did to me, expect for the exorcism. And mum left and took us with her a couple of months after the exorcism, she had it all planned. A friend of hers had rented a flat for us in Levin and mum got a job in a supermarket.'

'And she never reported it to the authorities, that your father abused you? She did nothing?'

'Whenever he hurt me, she'd say, "I can't do anything about it." And that was it. And after we moved away, she would never talk about it again, not once. That's when Carter and I became friends at school.' She smiled at Carter and said, 'His parents are so lovely – so normal, I love them. I spent a lot of time at their place right through high school.'

Lifting her wineglass and looking absently at it, she thought for a few moments and tried to sum up what she felt. 'Was he ever a good father? I don't know, maybe he was when I was very tiny, a baby. I can't remember any time when he seemed like a good father, someone I could trust - but how would I know what a good father is like?'

Liam looked slowly from her to Carter and back again. 'I think you know exactly what a good father is like – he would be just like Carter. Someone who's always looking out for you, who worries about you and tries to do everything he can to make your life easier – someone you know you can trust with your life.'

'Yes! That's it!' said Arapera and reached out to put her hand on Carter's. 'You're right, Liam, that's just how it would feel to have a good father.'

'What does Jackson look like,' asked Liam after a while. 'Does he look like your dad?'

Despite the traumatic topic, Arapera felt this conversation with silences and pauses, where nobody tried to break the mood by injecting an upbeat comment, was comforting. A conversation where feelings were respected and both men took care to work things through without rushing.

'Oh yes, they look just the same - blue eyes and brown hair, tall. I take after my mother.'

'You're just like her,' said Carter. 'To look at, I mean.' He smiled across the table at Liam. 'They're both so beautiful, and they have exactly the same colouring, but their personalities are poles apart. If anyone was abused in front of Arapera she'd never let it pass, she'd tackle anyone without hesitating. Quite fearless – always ready to defend kids at school against bullies like a fierce little warrior.'

'And where does the "poppet" come from?' asked Liam. 'It's intriguing to hear you use it.'

Carter shot Arapera a sideways glance. 'She used to protest but she's mostly given up now. When she first started coming to our house after school, my mum thought she was the cutest thing ever and she always called her poppet. So, I started doing it too and it kind of fitted the fake romance thing we had going at school. And it stuck.'

. . .

When Carter left after dinner to catch his train back to town, she knew that now he and Liam trusted each other there was no need to keep anything hidden from either of them and it made her feel happier than she could have imagined a few days ago.

I'm so lucky, she thought when she got into bed that night, because there can't be many women who have two such staunch men in their corner, and it kind of makes up for never having had a father-daughter relationship within my family. It's so good it probably makes up for having a disengaged mother as well.

The Soldierpilotpilot blog ((1012592 followers)
#revengeforthequeenofcool
#coolchick
#thequeenofcool

Today is going to be another instalment of the life and times of the Queen of Cool, because now things have escalated into the realm of malice and insanity.

Let's start with the malice. Someone, who is apparently called Daniel, has let himself be interviewed in the role of "anonymous, former date of the Queen of Cool" (the exact words in the article), possibly because she dumped him when he sent a very rude and unkind text about her to another woman. Revenge is always a powerful motivator, particularly when it pertains to the ego of a slighted male, who has been told where to go and put his nasty, deceitful self.

And of course, the offer of money is a motivator too. As if it wasn't enough that she got scammed by a bigamist, now the Queen of Cool has had a traumatic and deeply personal episode in her family life made public for someone's personal gain. Yes, I have it on good authority that Daniel got paid.

He told a journalist from a popular women's magazine a story about the Queen of Cool's father, that fire and brimstone preaching, deluded and angry man, who runs a second-hand car yard when he's not down on his knees praying for God to punish people. This unspeakable man took it upon himself to "know" that his 13-year-old daughter was possessed by a demon, subjected her to a home-made version of exorcism that defies description and amounts to torture, then beat her quite badly crying salty and self-pitying tears while he did so.

And how, I can hear you asking, do I know all this? Well, it's quite straight forward and involves no skulduggery (not my thing). A close and trusted friend of the Queen of Cool has told me why it had to be Daniel who sold the story. Because the Trusted Friend knew that the story Daniel sold had a made-up ending - the ending the Queen of Cool told Daniel, and only him, unable to tell him the true ending as it still had the power to reduce her to tears after all these years. And no, I will not tell you how it really ended after the beating, because I'm not like Daniel. I know how to keep a confidence and protect someone's privacy.

So, Daniel, here is a message for you: You are a self-serving, despicable creep and the Queen of Cool is well rid of you - you're not in her league. And if you want to embarrass yourself further, please get in touch and we can have a really frank chat about your character, and maybe you will do the decent thing and let me publish your full name. I do know it, but I have scruples of conscience. I realise you won't know what those words mean, but I'll explain them to you if you get in touch.

And why did her dreadful father think she was possessed by a demon? Because she had only recently started openly questioning his extreme religious beliefs, and this sign of incipient rebellion coincided with her being given a pink shoulder bag by her aunt. Her father proclaimed that the demon must have come with the bag, like a free gift from the manufacturer, and taken possession of this poor child.

And if these instances of malice and insanity were not enough, here is another example of why the human race possibly doesn't deserve to be saved. A couple, who migrates around the North Island in a house-bus, have issued a death threat against the Queen of Cool 'for taking liberties with witchcraft and damaging the reputation of the "Order of the Dark Arts". Well, I ask you, is that not the ultimate in craziness? What next? I despair of humanity; applying reason and logic never seems to change anything.

I have, of course, tracked down the person who gave me this information (I am now officially the Queen of Cool's one-man central intelligence agency), independently verified the facts and given all the information to the police; a second lot of data to join my first file about the bigamist.

But the good news is that there is an extradition request out for the man of multiple wives (still only two, whereof the Queen of Cool was the second) and things are slowly moving forward. I believe he owns a fancy condo on the Gold Coast, so maybe some money will make its way back to the Queen of Cool eventually.

We will return next time to the discussion about wind

turbines versus people's right to keep their views of pristine mountain ranges. There has been a great variety of comments on this topic - some of them are very interesting, others funny and some just selfish and outspokenly NIMBY, but all will be discussed.

Chapter 34

They had just finished lunch on the deck the next day, when the wind turned suddenly cold, threatening clouds appeared from the west, and they beat a hasty retreat inside. Now the rain was pounding down on the skylights and Essie was curled up on the sofa.

Arapera was sitting opposite Liam at the table studying an article about Georgian silver on an antiques website that Fiona had emailed a link to, "in case you're interested and want to know more, but no obligation, just if you want to", and Liam was quietly tapping away. Every now and then he paused and stared without focus through the rain splattered porthole glass with the quotation mark creases between his eyebrows.

'This is it,' he said after a while and swung his

laptop around for Arapera to look at. 'Tell me what to change or delete and then we'll publish it. There's no hurry, we can edit out anything you don't like.'

After Carter left the previous evening, they had stayed up late and discussed the detailed strategy, and now the moment had come.

She read the blog post twice, the second time very slowly, thinking of every word and what it might mean for Jackson, and how he would react to this being made public, so soon after he heard about it for the first time. To date she had only told four people about the exorcism and though their reactions were similar, this was the first time she herself had fully understood and accepted that her father's behaviour was more than just eccentric and harsh.

Talking to Liam, and listening when he and Carter discussed things, had clarified things in her mind and now she could see for herself that her father was a sick man, mentally ill and not just extreme in his beliefs, and it was as if someone had turned on the light in a dark room. How could I have deluded myself into thinking he's not mentally ill, she thought, how did I escape seeing it, even resisted the idea when Carter kept saying it? He's not just extreme and quick to anger and violence, he's sick, and as Carter and Liam both said, he's also very dangerous.

She looked across the table and said calmly, 'Publish it – it's perfect.' And when he looked surprised and pleased in equal measure, she reached across and curled her fingers around his.

'You're incredible, you really are. I'm so lucky to have you looking out for me. It's like having a personal bodyguard.'

'Good,' he said, and his eyes returned to the keyboard, but she could tell he was pleased; his voice hardly changed, but she knew he felt touched. Shutting her mind to thoughts about her father, she went back to the Georgian silver and how do decipher worn down hallmarks.

And then suddenly she remembered something Carter had said the day before and the feeling she had afterwards that she had missed something significant.

'What did Carter mean when he said I'd never have to tell anyone again? Was it just that you're the final person who needs to know? It felt kind of … significant.'

'I was just about to tell you about that.' Liam's expression was serious and perhaps slightly worried, and she realised there was something she had missed or not understood. 'Carter said he wanted to record the conversation – he told me while you were down here preparing lunch. He says you are suffering from unresolved PTSD and every time you talk about it, you aggravate the effect it has on you – kind of prolong the worst phase or re-start it. It's not that he doesn't realise that talking things over can be beneficial, but he thinks that repeating the story in detail takes it out of you, renews the damage, because you have never had any treatment. So, I said I would record it and tell you today, so you can delete it from my phone yourself if you want it gone.'

She was silent for so long that Liam's expression changed from possibly worried to openly concerned, as he sat silently watching her while she thought about it, and then she said decisively, 'No, let's keep it. He's right – having to tell the details is far worse than thinking about it as a memory. Re-telling it kind of makes it immediate and real, as if I have to start dealing with it all over again. So, leave it on your phone and if there should ever be some need for me – or you – to use it, at least I'll not have to go through it again.'

This is exactly the same thing that Caroline Hudson described, thought Arapera, the re-ignition that happens when you recall the actual event in your mind or tell someone, compared to recalling the memory of the event. With her eyes fixed on the picture of a Georgian claret jug without taking it in, she thought how odd it was that this chain of people and events and memories all fitted together somehow. It would be hard to try to explain it to someone else, this difference between recalling something and reliving it, though perhaps Liam would understand, if she tried to put it into words

. . .

It was very late when Arapera went to bed and though she was tired, she couldn't sleep. In the semi-dark, with the curtains pulled half-way across the porthole, she lay on her back and once again went through what Liam and Carter had said, what she had contributed then and since, and what Liam had written, and suddenly she started to cry.

Not just quiet tears running down her cheeks, but great heaving sobs that shook her body. The realisation that had finally entered her consciousness was so devastating, it was like physical assault. After a couple of minutes of sobbing into her pillow she wiped her eyes and her running nose on the edge of her T-shirt and got out of bed, stumbled across the main cabin and opened the door to Liam's bedroom. He sat up in bed and turned the light on, and she stopped in the doorway, simply stood there, silently wiping her tear drenched face with her fingers.

'What's wrong? What happened?'

'I just realised I ...' She couldn't find the words to explain it, she could barely understand it herself, this feeling that had overwhelmed her.

'I don't know how to ...' Her voice tapered off into silence.

Liam came around the bed and put his hands on her shoulders. 'Come and lie down - and don't worry about telling me now. We'll talk about it later – there's no hurry.'

'OK.' Arapera got into bed on the far side and lay on her back, unsure of why she had woken him up, why she had got into his bed and what she was going to say. This was such a strange situation and not something she had anticipated, but the impulse to go to him had been instinctive, not a reasoned decision, and now she felt deeply embarrassed.

After a while she cleared her throat and said quietly, 'It's just that I never realised that what he did to me was abuse – well, I did in a way, but what I mean is I didn't realise it made me a victim. Carter has always called it abuse, but I've never thought of myself as a victim – I thought I was strong, particularly in the way I managed to keep peace with him to avoid all the ranting and raving, and because I endured what he did to me. I just thought he was odd - and extreme. And without kindness, hard. It's only just sunk in tonight that I'm a victim.'

'Do you think your mother understood what he was doing when he performed that so-called exorcism?'

'Oh yes, that's why she stayed upstairs all that time. When she came down at the very end, she saw me lying naked, face down on the floor in the kitchen soaking wet, I saw her feet in the doorway, but I didn't dare raise my head. She heard him tell me I had to stay there all day and they would just walk around me as if I wasn't there, … she didn't help me, she just went back upstairs. They both made me a victim. He because of what he did, and she because she left me, lying there in agony, freezing cold and wet.'

She stopped to catch her breath; the concentration required to explain it was so intense that she nearly forgot to breathe. 'I think I got upset just now because I'd never thought of myself as a victim before.' She half sobbed and half laughed. 'I'm not a victim type person – that's what I would have said, before tonight.'

Liam turned on his side, pulled her closer and put his arm over her body, anchoring her against him. She sighed and closed her eyes, exhausted by the storm of emotion.

'You are the most amazing girl I've ever met,' he said with his mouth close to her cheek. 'I've never known anyone like you, so strong and calm and together – after all you've been through. You were seriously abused by a cruel, extremist parent, but he failed to cow you, and you've grown up to be a wonderful, strong woman. The fact that you never thought about yourself as a victim then, doesn't make you a victim now. You're a survivor, a strong survivor.'

Without responding she fell asleep like that and slept until dawn, when she woke up, still held against him and she turned under his arm and whispered, 'I love you, Liam.'

She could tell he was awake now; her whisper had roused him, and his breathing had changed, but he said nothing, and she wondered if the half-asleep impulse to tell him had been a huge mistake and ruined everything about this very new relationship. Then he moved his arm and put his hand on her cheek, cupping the side of her face in a gesture so tender that she felt her heart melting, and she knew.

'Are you sure it's not just because I've kind of rescued you? I'm so much older than you.'

She tilted her head so she could see his face properly in the early dawn light and make sure he was looking straight into her eyes.

'You mean like eleven years and three months and four days older? That has nothing to do with it, nothing! And neither do the circumstances of why I'm here. That you've given me sanctuary and helped me has nothing to do with it either. I've missed you since the day I lay under that car, and you talked to me while we waited. When things were going wrong at work and when people became intrusive about the accident and the ghosts – every single time I wished I could find you. I knew that if I could talk to you, I would feel different, anchored in some way and back to the real me.'

His gaze was steady on her face for a moment, then the corner of his mouth quirked up. 'Am I your rock to stand on in the maelstrom of life?'

'Yes, you are - exactly that.' She gave a little choke of laughter. 'And how the heck do you come up with a phrase like that - at *dawn* - and when someone's just told you they love you? And you haven't answered yet.'

'It's a quote, but I can't remember who said it. Just something that felt right. Of course, I love you, but I couldn't tell you, in case you just wanted to come here for a reprieve and to feel safe. No way was I going to complicate that for you. But I've loved you from the moment you so politely told me about your name – who else would be so courteous while stuck under a car? Only the Queen of Cool.'

A rapera opened her eyes and knew without checking that she was alone. This was the first time she had seen Liam's bedroom in daylight and after looking around she smiled, satisfied that her initial assessment of him was right; everything tidy, no clutter, the wardrobe door closed and nothing apart from two books and a torch on his bedside table. She lay on her back without moving and looked up through the skylight at clear blue sky. Mid-morning, she thought, I've slept in. She lay there quietly thinking back to the events of the night; the emotional melt-down that appeared seemingly out of nowhere, stumbling thought the main cabin to Liam's bedroom, waking beside him at dawn and telling him she loved him. It was surreal to think it only happened just a few hours ago. She smiled to herself as fragmented memories of love-making and quiet talking played back in her head, and then Liam appeared in the open door.

'Breakfast first or shower first?'

'Shower, please,' said Arapera, and Liam turned without coming into the room. She got out of bed, pulled her T-shirt over her head and headed for the bathroom. Liam was standing with his back to her at the kitchen bench, but he didn't turn around and warning lights flashed in Arapera's mind. This was not what she had expected, not after the way he had made love to her such a short time ago. Puzzled, she stood in the shower relishing the hot water streaming over her while she tried to work out what was going on, but there were only two realistic explanations: either he was regretting what had happened and worried about what her expectations might be, or he felt uncertain about how serious she was. She dried herself slowly and took her time squeezing the water out of the ends of her long hair with the towel, absentmindedly watching her face in the mirror. The prospect of a whole day with this uncertainty hanging over her like a silent threat, possibly until evening when it would either resolve itself at bedtime or continue to plague her, was unbearable. I must sort this out right now, she thought and nodded at her reflection, always best to know the worst first.

When she opened the bathroom door, Liam was just putting two slices of bread in the toaster, and though he turned around, he didn't look directly at her.

'Do you want me to leave?' she asked, keeping her voice as relaxed and casual as she could, desperate not to not sound anxious or needy. Avoiding making him feel he was under any obligation was uppermost in her mind, giving him the option of backing out of this situation without drama. *The way we do most things*, she thought, *calmly and in control of our emotions*.

His eyes met hers, and she couldn't even guess what he was thinking, the shutters were down; this might turn into something that would break her heart

'Would you like to leave? If you do, I'll drive you into town after breakfast.' His voice calm and nearly casual, but not quite as laid-back as he wanted it to sound. She sensed an undercurrent of something, a nearly unnoticeable tension.

Studying his face and seeing the little signs she knew so well by now, she sensed that he was worried and uncertain. It was like a current of cold air flowing around her body. She saw the little creases at the corners of his eyes, the two between his eyebrows, and she knew what she needed to do.

'Of course, I don't want to leave! I just thought last night might have been a bit … sudden, taken you by surprise.' She gave him a little smile, hoping this would defuse the sensation of possibly imminent disaster. 'I did invade your bedroom after all – it's not as if you invited me. I wouldn't want to you to feel ambushed into something you don't feel comfortable with.'

There was silence between them for a long moment, as they stood there looking at each other, he dressed and she with wet hair and only dressed in a T-shirt, neither of them revealing the full extent of their feelings. Then the corner of Liam's mouth tweaked up and he said, still with no particular emphasis, 'I'll tell you what I *really* want. If I had my way, you would stay here forever, live here with me and never go anywhere without me, apart from going to work. But I don't expect you to make a big commitment at this stage – you probably need to feel you're back in normal balance before you decide.'

The toast popped up and lightheaded with relief, she walked around him, got two plates out of the cupboard above the bench and said casually, 'You'd have to issue me with a trespass notice to get rid of me, Liam. This isn't a feeling that swept over me after that melt-down in the night. I've known what this was for weeks now, and it's not going to change.'

His arms came around her from behind and he chuckled. 'You are the Queen of Cool, no doubt about it. Would you please put those plates down and turn around so I can kiss you?'

'Breakfast on the deck of a boat with sunshine on the water,' said Arapera half an hour later. 'My God, it's paradise – apart from this damn cap.' She gave Liam a mock ferocious glance. 'And you have *no* idea what a mess my hair is going to be after drying all scrunched up like this — I'll look like a wild woman from the jungle.'

He laughed. 'Who could resist a wild woman? Not me — but to get serious for a moment, why did you never turn to your mother's family for help? I mean about how your father treated you. I've thought about it a lot since I heard the whole exorcism story.'

Arapera bent down to stroke Essie, who was wrapping herself around her ankles. 'It's a long story - and maybe a sign of our times. The family that never was. When my mum went to the UK at nineteen, she left behind a splintered whanau — her parents, my grandparents weren't on speaking terms with the rest of the relations on either side. I've never known why, and I've never asked. It must have been something awful because the rift never healed. Mum went to England and met my father, and her parents and two brothers went to live in Australia, and they've lived in Perth ever since. I saw my grandparents eighteen months ago, just after my divorce debacle, when Jackson hired a condo at a beach outside Brisbane, and they flew across to join us — my cash funds were low at the time. Jackson and I hadn't seen them for so long, but my mum's been to Perth twice, I think, or maybe three times. As far as I know, my grandparents haven't been back to New Zealand a single time in all those years. And I've never even met those two uncles in Western Australia or their families.'

Chapter 36

Late afternoon Arapera looked up from her corner of the sofa. 'Hey! Are you in the middle of a sentence or can I talk?'

She knew Liam would answer whenever she said something, but she had set a rule for herself about not starting conversations when he seemed preoccupied. His work was researching facts, writing his blog, and debating with those who commented. An onlooker might just see man just sitting in front of a laptop, looking absently out the porthole by his left shoulder, but it was his work and how he earned a living.

'Fine with me,' said Liam. 'I was just thinking I need to verify the facts I just read about the pace of rainforest destruction — some articles tend to repeat things without checking and I think the one I just read has old data.'

'So, should I tell Carter that I'm staying here?'

'You'll have to, won't you? Soon he'll start to wonder when you're coming back. Or don't you want to tell him quite yet, but you feel you should?'

'Oh no, I'm fine with telling him – just double checking, I suppose, that you're really OK with this forever arrangement you mentioned this morning.'

Liam got up, walked across the cabin and stood looking thoughtfully at her for a moment, then he sat down sideways on the sofa, just beside her bare feet. He picked up her left foot and held it firmly with both hands and a warm current ran up her leg. She stared into his eyes, mesmerised and silent, and he said, 'Arapera Woodhill, will you marry me?'

'Of course, I'll marry you,' she said and started to laugh. 'I thought you'd never ask, as they say. But there's one condition.'

'Here it comes – conditions, now! You don't want to live on a boat?'

'Don't be silly, I love living on a boat. But I have this old-fashioned principle that I don't accept marriage proposals from anyone whose surname I don't know.'

'You don't know?' He sounded genuinely surprised, then he started to laugh too. 'Really?'

'Well, how could I?' she said reasonably. 'Your real identity is so well concealed - how would I have found out? And you never told me at the start, you just said your name was Liam. Maybe you're not really called Liam at all – maybe you're a Tobias or a Sebastian.'

'Liam Whitlock – no middle name. Born in New Plymouth, orphaned at seventeen, two siblings – a sister in Hungary and a brother in Westport. They're both older than I am.'

'Oh, Liam,' said Arapera. 'How sad – losing your parents at seventeen. How did you cope?'

'You're so different,' said Liam instead of replying to her question. 'Everyone, and I mean literally everyone, who ever found out my parents died when I was a teenager, have asked "what happened?" I can't remember anyone ever reacting initially so differently – until just now. You are unique, there's nobody like you.'

'So, how did you cope? Seventeen, still at school?'

Absentmindedly, he rubbed her foot as he replied, and she loved the feeling of his warm hands on her skin. Not the same feeling as when Carter fixed the bandage around her ankle, she thought, there was no way of defining it, it was just different. She leaned back against the big cushion and listened, and Liam continued holding her foot while he told her about their home being sold, his siblings moving away to study and work, and how he spent two years with his uncle and aunt before he joined the army.

'So, your young cousin, the one who read that time-slip book you wrote about - is she the daughter of the uncle and aunt you lived with before the army?'

'Yes, she is, but she came later – she was a surprise parcel, completely unexpected, like she was delivered by a stork on the front step. My aunt who was rather chubby anyway, didn't realise she was pregnant until she felt the baby kicking – she thought she was past that kind of thing.' He laughed at the expression on Arapera's face. 'It's true, it happens. So, Melinda arrived while I was in the army, and she instantly became the most adored child in the universe. Her cousins and her siblings are all fifteen or twenty years older, or more - like a crowd of uncles and aunts, hellbent on spoiling her and telling her she's wonderful. Which she is.'

'Do you think you're the only one she talks to about all the films and books? Are you her favourite?'

'I don't know about being the favourite, but I know I'm the only one who lets her tell me the entire stories of romantic teenage films – I'm apparently the only one who doesn't interrupt her and say it sound like a very silly story.' He grins. 'Which they mostly are, of course, but not to her. Our WhatsApp or Zoom session sometimes last an hour or more, so you'll have to get used to it. Or I can let her talk to you about them, you might know some of the same things?'

Arapera was back on the sofa after a long walk with Liam on the Harakeke walkway in showers alternating with sunshine.

'Thank heavens you have more than one all-weather jacket – I never thought of asking Carter to bring mine. I thought you were over-cautious when you suggested taking rain jackets – did you know it was going to rain or was it just a good guess?'

'I had a feeling it might – there's a strong south-westerly coming in from the Tasman, and there were clouds on the horizon, and the island doesn't always protect us. Do you want to invite Jackson to come when he's got some free time – or perhaps we could go to Linton and meet him there. I'd like to get to know him.'

'He wants to come here – to inspect you.' Arapera picked up her phone from the coffee table and scrolled though messages. 'He sent a text yesterday. Here it is, listen to this: Carter says this Liam guy is the one from the accident videos lying beside the car. Amazing guy from what C says. Would love to meet him. Can I come for a visit next Sunday? I could take the bus. Just sold the car to a mate.'

'Invite him to spend the day here – we'll find something to do and if there's no transport in the evening, we can drive him back. Or he can spend the night – whatever fits with his schedule. Is he trained for a trade?'

'I can't remember what his job is, not the official name, I mean, but he's basically a mechanic – army vehicles of various kinds. I'm sure he'd love to tell you what he does, in great detail.' She put the phone back on the table and held out her coffee mug. 'If you're making another coffee for yourself, could you make me one too?' She laughed at herself. 'One swift step from flatting with a superb cook to living with a man who can barely make coffee and toast. How are we going to survive? I'm terrible at cooking, it's so boring.'

'Don't forget the scrambled eggs – one of my few skills in the kitchen.' Liam reached for her mug. 'And I've survived all these years on my own, so obviously we're not going to starve to death. Jackson might enjoy the engine room – it's piece of ancient machinery, but it works fine, and it's got some interesting quirks. Bet he's never seen anything like it.'

'I know what I was going to ask you the other day when you mentioned the bike and walking tracks - you said in your blog you might sell your mountain bike? Where is it?'

He grinned. 'I never had one, I prefer walking – it was just a thing I put in the blog, a pretend rhetorical question about how to pay that crazy woman, just to demonstrate that I was prepared to sacrifice something for the information she might have. To show that I would have done anything it took, if my other plan didn't work.'

'Would you have actually paid her ten thousand? I can't believe it!'

'Of course, I would have paid her. I was on a mission, and it seemed to be the only way of getting the story out of her if the charm offensive didn't work.'

Arapera studied his face for a long moment before she said, 'You truly are amazing – and I hope I can live up to the value you seem to have put on me and my life. It's a bit daunting, Liam!'

That made him laugh. 'I haven't put a value on you – don't be silly, it's impossible! I can't imagine what you're worth in money. But I did put a value on the info I might get – I was so damn determined to punish that scumbag you married that the price seemed unimportant.'

Chapter 37

What had been a promising spring morning with a warm and gentle breeze, had changed after lunch, The wind came up strong and a bit cooler, so Arapera put a sweatshirt over her T-shirt to walk to the supermarket. After a discussion, that some might have called a negotiation, Liam had backed down and said he was probably over cautious in insisting he went with her everywhere. But now, walking back mid-afternoon with her shopping, it was calm and she was rapidly getting too hot. She briefly considering stopping and taking one layer off but decided it was too much trouble and continued with shopping bags in both hands.

What is it with supermarkets? she thought and hitched her bag higher on her shoulder. I nearly always buy more things than those on my list, it must be the way they display tempting things at eyelevel. She groaned when her phone buzzed with a call, but hoping it was Jackson, she put the bags on the pavement and just managed to get her phone out in time to answer. A quick glace showed her it was Fiona, not something she had expected.

'Hi,' said Fiona cheerfully. 'How are you doing on that barge? Is it comfortable?

'It's very comfortable,' she replied cautiously, as if anything might happen next, because this was unexpected and confusing. 'How did you know where I am?'

'Oh, don't worry! I haven't been spying, but when I discovered you were the girl who ended up under that car in town, which I did after you came to the house, I mentioned it to a friend of mine. I said I'd just employed that girl, and I'd noticed the limp, but I never asked what had happened to your foot.' She chuckled. 'And would you believe it, he put me on to that blog and told me he knows the blogger - small world! And what a story!'

Arapera smiled to herself because this explained something she had wondered about. 'Liam told me someone had mentioned that I got a new job – someone who was pretty vague, he didn't know what the job was, just that it was about IT for a private company. Your friend is obviously very discreet about your business.'

'Oh, he hasn't got a clue,' said Fiona casually and Arapera could hear the smile. 'Like most of my friends

- they don't know any details at all. You know what I'm like about security. The neighbours think is a seed business and my friends, or most of them, think I just do forensic accounting jobs from home. If they come to the house, I tell them I've got a tenant in a granny flat out the back - if they comment on the shed, I mean. And I say it was there when I bought the house.'

She paused and muttered 'oh, bugger' under her breath. 'Sorry, another tight corner, another cloud of dust. And tell your friend Liam that I haven't mentioned him to anyone, so officially I know nothing about him or his barge or anything. The guy who told me has sworn me to silence about Liam's name, and he trusts me. We've been mates for years – we get together sometimes, just for a nice evening with good wine and occasional sex, you know, nothing serious.'

Arapera laughed at this unexpected display of casually intimate honesty and thought that Fiona was the most surprisingly multi-faceted person she had ever known. With some difficulty she managed to pick up both shopping bags in one hand and resumed walking. 'So, you don't even know Liam's surname then?'

'No, just his first name – ouch!' said Fiona.

'Are you OK? Where are you? And what is it that keeps happening, it sounds painful?'

'Oh, I'm fine, just bumped my other thigh on the corner of a table, I'll be covered in bruises before I get out of this place. I'm in a *very* interesting second-hand shop just on the outskirts of Mount Isa, fabulous. I hope you can hear me - I'm keeping my voice low now, so the owner doesn't hear me rave or the prices will mysteriously double or treble. They've been buying up all kinds of Victorian and Edwardian stuff from the original settlers all over the district for years and years. You know, families clearing out granny's house when she died and that sort of thing. I've never seen such a crowded shop - they probably buy house lots as we call them. I've found a few Georgian things too, and by the look of it they buy a lot more than they sell. I'm going to buy forty or fifty pieces, I think, perhaps more. I think I'll be an interior decorator today, or maybe I'll be looking for props for a TV drama.' She laughed. 'My life is full of deception, isn't it – but you can trust me, I promise. There's stuff here that's so dusty you can't tell if it's glass or silver. I'm filthy – must have moved half a ton of stuff in four rooms so far to find out what's hidden behind things they acquired later.'

In the back of Arapera's head an internal conversation about how much to say was going on while she listened to Fiona, and now she said, 'I'm staying here, on the boat – forever - with Liam.' And then she realised how Fiona might take the news and added quickly, 'But I'll be working for you, don't worry. The boat is in the Mana marina, and I'll just take the train to town most of the time. I thought I'd go in my running gear and run up to your place, perhaps leave some extra clothes there?'

'Wow!' said Fiona and chuckled again. 'You're a

fast worker, aren't you? I must meet Liam as soon as I get back, this is the most exciting thing I've heard in a long time. My friend, who told me you were on a boat, he was pretty tight-lipped about this Liam character. All he said was he knew where you were and what had happened to you. I like the blog.'

This is very funny, thought Arapera as she walked through the gates to the marina, it's like jigsaw pieces of information gradually coming together. She hasn't mentioned the videos, so maybe she read the blog and didn't look up those videos.

'Here's the best bit,' she said. 'You said you read Liam's blogs about the accident? Did you check out the videos online? No? Well, do watch them and you'll see Liam lying on the ground beside the car keeping me sane – and occasionally standing up.'

'Jesus! It gets better and better, like a hero rescuing a damsel in distress – I love it. I must meet this guy, let's have dinner in town or something when I get back.'

'Or you come here, it's such a lovely boat, I want you to see it. I'll stop now, I've been walking back from the supermarket while we've been talking, but I'm at the boat now. And if you decide you trust Liam, maybe you'll let me tell him about the shed? It would be so hard to work for you and not be able to talk to him about it.'

'Oh yes – that would be impossible.'

• • •

'When you've finished writing, I'd like to tell you about the chat I had with Fiona on the way back from the supermarket,' said Arapera when the shopping was stowed away and she had turned the electric jug on.

'I've finished for now.' Liam got up and stretched his arms up, his hands flat against the low ceiling. 'It's taking longer than usual but getting asked to write a five-hundred-word column for The Listener made me very aware of how I put things.'

'Do you think it will become a regular thing?'

'I've no idea – which is one reason I'm taking so much care with this one. Perhaps it's a test and if they like it, they might ask for more. Did you buy some more biscuits?'

Arapera laughed. 'Of course, I bought more biscuits! How would you cope without biscuits? So anyway, I thought you'd like to meet her – Fiona, I mean. The story about how she first found out about my accident and about me being here is very complicated. We could go to town and have dinner with her, or she could come here, if you don't mind. And I've just realised I never told you about her properly.'

Liam took the mug she handed him and reached for the packet of biscuits. 'Let's invite her for dinner when she's back from her trip. Obviously, I must get to know her if you're going to work for her. Come and sit down and tell me what she said.'

'So, listen to this,' said Arapera after telling the

story about the treasure trove in the Mount Isa shop. 'I've had a great idea for when I start working for Fiona. Her place is in Aurora Terrace, which is about two and half kilometres from the Wellington railway station – I measured it on Google Earth - so I thought I'd take the train from here, dressed in my running gear, put whatever else I need in a little backpack – which I'll have to buy – and then run to her house.'

'You'd really like to run there and back every day? Think of the rain in the winter and there won't be a bus service to her part of town, I wouldn't think.'

'But I normally run every day anyway, whatever the weather. It's just that you don't like running, you'd rather walk, so you think it's weird. But I'm the opposite and running in the rain is normal for me just like going for walks in the rain is normal for you. Running keeps you warm, walking doesn't.'

'So far you've really only told me that besides the IT part of the job you'll be dispatching precious item to buyers all over the world, so what is Fiona's business?'

'Five separate business entities,' said Arapera and pulled the biscuits closer to her end of the coffee table. 'If you eat any more of those, you'll have to go back to the shops yourself. All five deal in precious or desirable things but of different kinds. Silver, crystal, rare books, jewellery etc. All kept in a huge, long shed that's built like a giant safe with every security measure you can imagine – behind her house. And, yet another business, forensic accounting, which I'd never heard about before.'

'Oh good,' said Liam and leaned over to pull the biscuits back to his side. 'That's very convenient, so you've got something to tell people about what she does, so her shed can continue to be a secret. You're very analytical so you'd fit in well as her forensic assistant too. And I'd love to hear more about the kind of jobs she does, it sound interesting.'

When Arapera looked up from her book a couple of hours later the sun was still shining and the sound of wind in the rigging on the yachts had stopped. 'I'm getting used to the changes in weather – it's a bit like Wellington which I hadn't expected. Somehow, I thought the Mana coast was always sunny. I'll make dinner now and perhaps we can eat on the deck before it gets too chilly.'

Liam watched her for a few moments as she opened the fridge and started assembling ingredients. 'What are you making?'

'As you know I'm a terrible cook, but I think it's time I did something domesticated around here, so I'm going to try something Carter makes sometimes. That's why I bought all these extra things when I was in the supermarket. I texted him yesterday and asked for a shopping list for his stir-fry special.' She laughed. 'He couldn't believe it. He thinks you've hypnotised me or sprinkled magic dust over me.'

Coming to stand beside her, Liam studied the ingredients laid out on the bench. 'You don't have to cook, you know - we can do what I've been doing for years. Buy Chinese or pizza or frozen meals or go out and eat. I don't want you to feel you have to become a great cook or any kind of cook at all. You have so many talents already there's no need to add another.'

Arapera laughed and jabbed him lightly in the ribs with her elbow. 'Don't worry, I'm not planning to become the great housewife – but I thought learning to do one or two, or maybe even three, of Carter's favourite dishes would be nice to vary things with. The only thing I'm good at is making cauliflower with cheese sauce.'

Chapter 38

The shout came from behind Arapera and made her jump, but she knew who it was without looking. A loud voice called out, 'Ahoy, Stillwater! Permission to board?' and she rolled her eyes at Liam, who laughed and got to his feet.

'I might not be able diverted her this time, so prepare yourself,' he said in a low voice before he turned to their visitors. 'And how are you two?'

Margaret and Sinbad, the latter with his captain's hat on and his white beard looking more luxuriant than ever, were now on the pier right beside the Stillwater's short gangplank.

'Come and have a drink. We've just finished dinner,' said Liam. 'Ara bought some lovely cheeses today – we'll open a nice red to go with them.'

'Let's move inside, it's getting chilly again,' said Arapera and busied herself with plates and glasses, while in her head she considered what Margaret would ask this time. Last time the questions got nowhere due to Liam's great intervention of bringing out the Scrabble game and challenging them to try and beat his and Arapera's joint points. And all without even checking if I'm good at Scrabble, she thought now, so funny - I could have been hopeless at it or not known the rules, it was pure luck we won.

With wine glasses in front of them and a platter of cheese and biscuits, the interrogation started immediately. Catching Liam's amused glance out of the corner of her eye, Arapera ignored him and concentrated on Margaret.

'So, you're still on leave, then? Or are you staying?' asked Margaret as she reached for the crackers. 'I suppose there are lots of jobs going in Wellington. What is it you do?'

Arapera felt relieved that the first question at least was easy to answer and smiled at Margaret who regarded her surprisingly intently.

'I'm staying - I just got a job in town, but it's not starting for another month or so. And meanwhile I'll get my clothes and things moved.'

Sinbad was telling Liam something about his boat, and Margaret continued without pause, ignoring the men. 'Is it good job? What is it you do?'

'I've mainly been working in the IT industry, programming and a lot of analytical work, but the new job is as an assistant to a forensic accountant.' That will side-track her from my private life, thought Arapera, but Margaret proved her wrong.

'That sounds intriguing, you'll have to tell me more about it later. And where are your parents? Are they in Auckland?'

'No, some of my family live in the South Island and some live in Perth.' Arapera decided to take a liberty with the truth to avoid having to discuss her parents' divorce and whatever might follow on from that. Hoping that an information dump would exhaust the subject, she continued. 'My grandparents and my two uncles live in Perth too and my brother is in the army here in New Zealand, at Linton. I have an aunt on my father's side who lives not too far away, so I'll be able to visit her more often.'

Maybe that will shame her into stopping asking me things, she thought, and just then Liam turned to Margaret and cast a slanting glance at Arapera who saw the corner of his mouth tweak up and knew he was enjoying this charade. 'Ara is superbly qualified, she'd get a job in five minutes anywhere. Not only pretty, but smart too.'

'I *still* feel I've seen you somewhere.' Margaret was now on another quest. 'I didn't notice the first time we met – at that café - probably because you were wearing a cap, but the other day when we came by, I said to Sinbad afterwards that you remind me of someone, but I can't think who it is.'

'Lily Collins,' said Liam decisively, taking Arapera

completely by surprise. 'It's what I thought the first time I met her. She's the spitting image of Lily Collins, the actress.' And then he laughed. 'And I only know this because Melinda – remember my young cousin who came to stay a couple of months ago? You met her, too, in the café. She and I watched a film together called Inheritance, a thriller that Lily Collins is in. She's the daughter of Phil Collins.'

'I *love* Phil Collins!' Margaret was instantly diverted. 'Remember *Take a look at me now* when he performed at that huge outdoor concert, the audience went wild, tens of thousands of them - I wonder if he's still alive?' And then Sinbad chipped in with the one-word exclamation, 'Genesis!' which promptly set Margaret off on more musical reminiscences until what had started this string of memories was safely forgotten.

'That was so clever of you,' said Arapera later that evening, when they tidied away the debris from the table. 'You completely diverted her, and she never got back to the question of where she might have seen me before. Not that I mind, but as you said before – the fewer people who know where I am for a while, the better. And you remembered to call me Ara, too! Did you hear anything new about the crazy witchcraft people?'

'No, but I'll check again tomorrow.' Liam closed the dishwasher and turned it on. 'I did ask the cops to keep me informed – I told them you were here with me after you came to stay, said I needed to know what was going on, but heaven knows if they will. They've probably got more pressing things to get on with.'

'Do Sinbad and Margaret know what you do for a living? I was worried I was going to be put on the spot if something came up. That woman never stops asking questions and she doesn't care how personal she gets.'

'Nobody here has any idea about what I do. I tell people I won Lotto and bought the boat and retired from being a pilot. Little did I know I'd ever meet a real Lotto winner. When it comes to my privacy, I have no scruples about telling lies. Particularly since the blog took off like a rocket – who knows what kind of crazies might want to come and punch me in the nose for some opinion I voiced. Not that I can't fight, but I'd rather not have blood on the deck and my marina reputation ruined.'

'I did tell Fiona because she already knew part of it – it kind of came out in amongst all the talking about her friend who told you I had a new job etc. When I've talked to Carmen since I've been here, I've just said I'm staying with my aunt – she's got no idea I know you. But I can tell you one thing right now – when she finds out I've deceived her she'll be furious for two seconds and then she'll be super excited. It was she and Ollie who first showed me the videos of the accident.

Chapter 39

The day of Jackson's visit was rainy after four days of glorious weather. 'God, I'm so disappointed,' said Arapera, after introducing him to Liam. 'We were going to take you on our favourite walk along the coast, but it's no fun in this weather.'

'I don't need to go for walks, I get so much exercise anyway – it's part of my daily life. I'd rather see the engine room if that's OK,' said Jackson and looked hopefully at Liam. 'Carter says I'm in for a treat. Oh, and I forgot to say - I'm getting a ride to Wellington airport next weekend for the engagement party. My sergeant is flying to Christchurch on leave and his flight leaves just after ours, so I won't have to bus down.'

'I should have asked you to come, too,' said Arapera to Carter on the phone an hour and a half later, looking across the room at Jackson and Liam sitting side by side at the table, studying the old engine maintenance manual that had come with the barge. 'You and I could have gone for that walk Jackson rejected. Jackson isn't going to let go of Liam until he's wrung every last bit of information about the engine from him, and I *think* I just heard him promise that he'll do anything that needs doing in future.'

'Just his kind of thing, greasy and complicated and hard work.' Carter chuckled. 'But isn't it great though – I mean for him and Liam to have something to kind of bond over. I wondered how they were going to get on. And by the way, I saw Carmen and Ollie last night, at the hospital.'

'Not another miscarriage – please!' said Arapera. 'Is she OK?'

'Oh, it wasn't her, it was Ollie – he got something in his eye, and he thought it was still there, said it had been there since the day before. But it was OK, he just felt the scratch it had made, so we gave him some antibiotic ointment and sent him home. They said they can't wait to see you and meet Liam.'

'Oh, good – I mean good that Carmen's OK. Did you tell them I'm here? I told Carmen I was staying with my aunt.'

'Yeah, I did – didn't realise she didn't know. She was very … let's say indignant at first that you hadn't told her.' Carter chuckled quietly. 'But she got more and more excited, so prepare yourself for a long talk to explain everything.'

The call from Carmen came half an hour later, as

if triggered by what Carter had told her, and was exactly what Arapera had imagined, but without the initial outburst about not having been told the truth. She's had time to get over it, she thought, as she listened to a stream of questions. Those explosive reactions, they are over in a flash, thank heaven.

'Carter said this guy lives on a boat – is it a big one? And where did you meet him? You never said a word! Honestly, Arapera – you're getting very secretive. First this new job that hasn't started, very mysterious and vague, and now a new guy on a boat! And I hear about it in ED from Carter! Is he a hunk?'

Arapera knew exactly what she meant, but she couldn't resist the temptation. 'Carter's always been a hunk - surely you know that - what a weird question.'

'Don't be an idiot, I mean this Liam guy. Is he a hunk?'

'Hang on,' said Arapera and with the phone still close to her face she called out across the cabin. 'Liam – sorry to interrupt but Carmen wants to know if you're a hunk.'

'I wouldn't think so,' he said looking slightly confused, but Jackson burst out laughing. 'Tell her he's hunkish enough –there's no need for her to worry you got yourself a wimp.'

'Did you hear that, Carmen? He's hunkish, says Jackson who's here for a visit.'

As soon as the call was over, she texted Carter. "Did you tell Carmen who Liam is? Or what he does?" and the reply came back a few minutes later "Of course not.'

Arapera was back in her corner of the sofa after making everyone a second cup of coffee. The conversation between Jackson and Liam had moved on to army vehicles, and she decided to leave them to it and returned to the novel she was reading on her Kindle, something Carter had recommended. She was relieved that Carter had not revealed what Liam did for a living. Not that she totally understood why he was keeping it so private, but whatever sat behind his decision, they must manage the balancing act of keeping him neutral in the eyes of those who didn't need to know.

Late afternoon, after Jackson had left to catch the bus back to the Linton army camp, Arapera texted Carter. "Very successful visit, conversation after finishing with the engine manual consisted mainly of acronyms and initials, LAV, IMV, LOB etc. Apparently all army vehicles that both guys are familiar with – super boring. Love the book you told me to read, never read anything so absorbing before and never read anything by John Irving, love it! How did you find him?"

When Carter's reply appeared on her phone, she laughed out loud. "I've been telling you for years how I keep getting locked in the library. Believe me now?"

Chapter 40

On the day of the engagement party Liam stopped outside Arapera's flat in Palmer Street and said, 'This is the exact spot I where I parked one of those days when I sat here watching your apartment block. I got here very early so I'd see any nutters turning up – and that's when I spotted Carter a couple of times.'

'Way beyond the call of duty, I must say – I'm amazed you did that.' Arapera reached over and put her hand on his, still finding it hard to believe he had been looking after her safety while she was completely unaware of him sitting out there in his car. 'And I was inside and had no idea, but I thought of you a lot, wished I could talk to you again. But tell me, how would you have known someone was a nutter? I'd think crazy people look just like everyone else – well perhaps not all of them, obviously not the ones wearing tinfoil hats. Or did you know who you were looking for?'

'No, I just reckoned anyone who hesitated before pressing one of the buttons on the door panel, as if they didn't know which one they wanted, stood there too long or ran their finger up and down the buttons, hesitating. Or maybe they'd just hang around outside the door, leaning against the wall and reading "Nutters Weekly". I felt obliged to do something constructive, and it was the only thing I could think of − I didn't have many options.'

'Here he comes, the Viking nurse.' Arapera waved her arm out the window to attract Carter's attention. 'So, we're on time so far. Now we'll just hope Jackson gets to the airport on time.'

'Hi, guys,' said Carter and started getting into the seat behind Liam and then got out again. 'Sorry, I'll come around to the other side'

'What was that all about?' Arapera tried to look at him over her shoulder. 'Is it so you can gaze at Liam's handsome profile?'

'You're very cheeky this morning, poppet, but no, not the temptation of Liam's profile - it's just that your seat is further forward, and I can sit here in comfort. Long legs can be a curse.' Then he laughed. 'Remember how my mum used to measure my growth and write it on the doorjamb to the dining room every birthday? Until one day she couldn't reach high enough to make the mark, and she had to get my dad to do it.'

'It's lovely to be going to the South Island again.' Arapera looked around the terminal and dropped her carry-on bag at her feet. 'I haven't been down south since your parents took us in the campervan that time, Carter. I think I was fifteen – it was the best holiday ever.'

'I wish they hadn't sold it.' Carter shook his head at his parents' lack of foresight. 'We could have taken it across on the ferry – I loved sleeping in the van, it was like a little house.'

'Really?' Liam laughed and looked Carter up and down. 'You're probably too tall now to fit – or you could be in the campervan and the rest of us would have a motel unit.'

'Oh shit!' said Carter quietly and Arapera swung around to see what he was looking at, alarmed by his tone. Her father was standing a short distance from them, slowly scanning the terminal, and she stood as if frozen, waiting to see what he would do when he noticed her. Then he spotted them and came towards them, his expression tight and angry. She knew that look, the way the veins on his temples would suddenly become engorged and his face would go dark red, the precursors to rage and punishment.

Carter and Liam both stepped forward, one on

each side of her and slightly blocked her just as her father reached them.

'You are not going! I will *not* allow you to not consort your whore of a mother!' His voice loud and angry, attracting the attention of people around them. Arapera was acutely conscious of a bubble of silence developing, of others stopping what they were doing or talking about, halting on their way through the terminal, faces turning in their direction.

'Mr Woodhill,' said Carter, 'please don't make a scene - and don't shout at Arapera.' His voice was calm, and he spoke kindly, but Arapera's father advanced and reached out as if to take hold of her. Liam and Carter closed the gap between them and effectively created a barrier between Arapera and her father, and Liam said, in a voice she had never heard him use before, a voice of confident command. 'Step back! Now!'

And it worked. In the tiny gap between the men shielding her Arapera watched her father take a step back and for a moment she thought he looked undecided, as if he might turn and walk away. She held her breath, willing him to leave, but he changed his mind. His face was suffused with anger now, his hands clenched into fists, and he advanced again until he stood nearly chest to chest with Liam. His mouth opened and she knew he was going to shout, to start one of his excruciating tirades of abuse and threat. She walked around Carter and stopped in front of him to face her father.

'Don't do this, dad,' she said, trying to keep her voice even and calm. 'People are staring and if you don't go quietly the security people will come and you will be in serious trouble.'

Out of the corner of her eye she saw Liam turning, but she had no attention to spare for him, she had to focus on trying to de-escalate her father's fury before this turned into a hideous spectacle, a public confrontation and possibly physical violence. Her father's face was now so red that even his eyes looked bloodshot, and he stuttered something she could not hear, as if he was losing the ability to form words. Before she realised that Carter had moved, he appeared beside her father, put his arm over his shoulder, and was talking quietly into his ear, gently but firmly moving him away to one side.

Arapera stood still for a moment, letting the tension ebb from her mind and body and then she turned slowly and carefully, feeling as if a sudden movement might unbalance her. She looked in the other direction, creating a separation between what had just taken place and the present. When she turned to look again, Carter had led her father to a row of seats a short distance away and was gently pushing her father's shoulder to make him sit down. Liam reappeared with Jackson beside him, and they stood silently watching the scene a few metres away. Now

Carter was holding one of her father's hands, still talking.

'He's taking dad's pulse,' said Jackson in a near whisper. 'What's wrong with him? He looks awful. Should I go over there?'

'No, stay here and let Carter handle it. He seems to have calmed your dad down quite a bit.' Liam put his arm over Arapera's shoulders and pulled her closer. 'Carter knows what he's doing, and we have plenty of time before we have to board.'

The little crowd that had formed around them had melted away and Carter stayed where he was, and even from a distance Arapera could see her father's stance relaxing. After a few minutes both men got to their feet and shook hands. Carter stayed where he was and watched Arapera's father disappear through the doors before he turned back and joined their little group again.

'Well done,' said Liam. 'That was quite a little chat you two had. Did you manage to convince him to leave Arapera alone?'

Jackson's eyes were fixed on Carter, and Arapera was sure her own looked just like his, expectant, half hopeful and half apprehensive.

'He's promised to go straight to his doctor,' said Carter. 'His pulse was one hundred and ninety when we first sat down, and that was after he'd already calmed down a bit - so we had a conversation about blood pressure extremes and strokes and heart attacks etcetera. He got scared when he realised how dangerous it was to get so angry, so I hope I've managed to persuade him to tell his doctor about his bouts of fury - and maybe his beliefs.' He made a face and shrugged. 'Hopefully they'll work through to a solution – at least for his blood pressure, but something to keep him calm too. It all depends on the doctor and how intuitive they are.'

Liam drove the hire car they picked up at the Marlborough airport with Jackson beside him holding his phone with the navigation app open and the sound on.

'That damn woman's voice,' said Jackson. 'I always feel as if I'm five years old when she tells us to turn in two hundred meters in that weird voice. I had a kindy teacher who sounded just like that, as if she had to speak very slowly and space the words out or you wouldn't understand - it made me feel stupid.'

'I think she's wonderful.' Carter smiled and looked sideways at Arapera. 'A bit like your sister when she tells me how to sort something out on my laptop, infinitely patient and kind.'

'Listen, Jackson,' said Arapera, after a second groan from her brother. 'Try to think of it like this - that woman spent hours and hours recording set phrases, like "at the next intersection" and "take the third exit" plus all the single words they needed. And then she spent a thousand hours recording every single place name *and* every single street name in the world! A lot of people think is an artificially created voice, but you can look up the name of that woman and check what she looks like. And then someone very smart wrote the code for picking out each word she needs to say and put them together in sentences, and it all happens while the satellite picks up how fast you're moving - and then you miss the turn, and she has to start over and redirect you onto the right path. It's a flipping miracle when you think of it, so just be grateful she's doing it for you for free!'

While the others laughed and Jackson said, 'Sorry, sorry, navigator lady!' Arapera's thought returned to the party ahead and meeting her mother and the handsome fiancé, a potential minefield of unforeseen ways of putting her foot in it or not reacting in the way her mother expected. Lots of smiles, she thought, say nothing very definitive, just act pleased and excited and hope for the best. In the back of her mind a range of unguarded comments that mustn't materialise have popped up. No comments on appearance other than to say her mother looks wonderful, no comments that could possibly be interpreted to reference the age difference, and definitely no comments that referred to her father. She looked up and met Liam's eyes in the rear vision mirror and thought how strange this was, and she was still not used to it, the way he seemed to sometimes sense what she was thinking. Though his mouth wasn't visible in his reflection she could tell he was smiling and smiled back.

'You have arrived at your destination,' said the woman on the navigator app and Jackson replied, 'Thank you!' very politely, which made Carter laugh.

'My God, it's as big as a two-storey house,' said Jackson when they walked into the motel unit Liam had booked. 'I didn't know you could get them as big as this. We could live here forever.'

'Three bedrooms and a living area plus a full kitchen we don't need. I thought it would be comfortable to have lots of space and privacy and nobody sleeping in the lounge.'

'Great dress!' said Jackson when Arapera came downstairs, changed and ready for the engagement party. 'Is it new?'

'God no, I've had it for three or four years – it's just that you never see me properly dressed up.'

Liam, who had already seen it in their bedroom, now looked her up and down again and said, 'Gorgeous and smart, as always. Never met anyone like her before.'

'Really?' Jackson sounded nearly insulting, but she knew he didn't mean it like that. 'Never?'

And Liam did one of those things he sometimes did, suddenly deadly serious and very deliberate.

'Jackson, it's the honest truth – your sister is the most amazing woman I've met in my life.'

They arrived at the vineyard after a minor detour when Carter suddenly had an idea there was a shortcut after checking the Google map on his phone, but it turned out to be a dead-end road that ended at a gate to a paddock full of sheep. Backtracking towards town, Arapera exclaimed, 'Oh heavens! Engagement present? Are we supposed to bring a present?'

They all looked at each other and it turned out nobody knew. 'I've never been to an engagement party before,' said Liam. 'It's not like a wedding, is it? But I have no idea what's expected.' And neither did Jackson, of course, so they did another detour and found a lovely gift shop where they bought a dozen retro wineglasses.

'Maybe it's coals to Newcastle, but you can't go wrong with wineglasses,' said Carter confidently. 'You can never have too many, and these are gorgeous – bound to be far more glamourous that the winery glasses from the tasting room they probably use all the time.'

'Whatever your mum asks you, just say yes and do it. Whatever it is – request from Juan,' said Liam in a quiet aside to Arapera an hour later and moved a few steps to the left where Jackson was talking to a girl, and she watched him presumably saying the same thing to Jackson, when the girl turned to study the canapes on the table behind her. He glanced at Arapera with a slight smile and made a 'stay here' gesture before he walked towards the two large doors that opened out onto a terrace with tables and chairs, where Juan joined him. Side by side they walked across the lawn and out between the rows of vines and she watched them, curious and intrigued. Juan was obviously doing the talking, gesticulating as they walked further and further away, as if towards the distant hill at the end of the vineyard, and Liam listened, head at an angle.

Arapera turned back towards the bar where parcels and cards were now piled up and her mother stood surrounded by guests, talking and laughing. It's like a personality transplant, she thought, and studied her mother's animated face, or perhaps this person was hiding inside her for a couple of decades, waiting for the right environment to emerge like a butterfly. Maybe this is what she was like before dad revealed his mad religious side? It's unreal to see her like this, so different – as if she's not my mum any longer, she's a new person called Linda.

'What a transformation!' Carter appeared beside her and followed her gaze. 'I can't get over it – I keep looking at her and thinking she's been switched for a body double, a younger double. And I didn't realise she'd gone back to her maiden name. I went to call her

Mrs Woodhill like I always used to when we were at school, but she cut me off and told me to just call her Linda and said she's gone back to her maiden name. Obviously she's got more friends now than she did back then – I can't get near her to have a proper conversation.'

'I only managed to talk to her for a couple of minutes myself and then that hoard came in en masse and I moved away. I was just about to join Jackson over there and get myself another glass of wine.'

'Hey, did Liam give you some cryptic warning about saying yes to mum?' asked Jackson a moment later. 'What was that all about? He said it was a message from Juan.'

Carter shook his head. 'I wonder what's going on because I got told to say yes, too. And now I've just spotted those two, way out there among the vines.'

Th men were standing facing each other a good distance from the vineyard buildings, and Juan was clearly still talking, his hands emphasising what he was saying.

The three of them watched for a moment and then looked at each other blankly, and Jackson laughed. 'We'll do what we're told, and then Liam will fill us in. That's a very long conversation going on out there, so I can't wait to hear what it's all about. Did you realise Juan's a real catch? His parents *own* this place – they've been here for about twenty years.'

'Do they? I had no idea. How did you find that

out?' Arapera felt slightly disconcerted at the news, as if it was the final straw, the drop that would cause the cup of surprises to run over. 'And which ones are the parents?'

'Some girl told me – just a minute ago. She works here too – where they make the vine, can't remember what the job is called.'

'Vintner, perhaps,' said Carter. 'Check out the exotic looking guy about sixty-five or so – just to the left of that potted palm on the terrace. That's the father, Mr Alonso – and I guess the mother is the matron with the fabulous necklace just a bit further back from Linda, beside the tall bald guy. She looks kind of Spanish.'

'This is weird,' said Jackson. 'It's like mum's been having a whole new life down here and we had no idea. She's not great at communicating, is she?'

'It might be more that she's been too busy,' said Arapera. 'I wonder if she got this job and then hooked up with Juan, or if she's working here because of him. I can't wait to hear what Liam and Juan are talking about – they've been out there for ages now.'

Chapter 42

It was half past eleven when Liam parked outside their motel unit. 'Let's bring a bottle from that box inside,' he said. 'It was very generous of Juan to give us a whole dozen, just because I told him I liked the white they had for those who didn't want bubbly. We'll sit down and have another glass of wine and I'll tell you the whole story – one of the best I've ever heard.'

'I've been waiting hours for this.' Carter shook his head as he went around to get the wine out of the back. 'Not the wine, the story. I've never known anyone who could hold on to a story so long, Liam. Weren't you dying to tell us?'

'You wait – it's not the kind of tale I could start telling in that crowd. But wine first!'

'OK,' said Carter a few minutes later and slumped back in an armchair. 'God, it's exhausting talking to so many new people – don't know what it is. Possible it's because of how you have to feel your way, find out what they're about, find a topic that kind of fits.'

'I thought you were used to from the emergency room,' said Liam. 'You must be constantly talking to strangers.'

'Totally different, though – there they know my role and I use it in certain ways to find out what I need to know. I can't do that in a social context. But I enjoyed Juan's dad – he's very friendly, told me why they decided to leave Spain and about the ceremony when they got their New Zealand citizenship – lovely guy.'

'So, here it is,' said Liam, clearly relishing the moment. 'He took me aside right away when we arrived, just for a moment, and said I was the older male, obviously trusted and could I please pass that warning to all of you as soon as possible without attracting attention. Which I did, of course, because he was clearly on a mission. And he said to meet him on the terrace when I'd told you all, and we'd go for a walk so he could explain. I mean, how could I possible refuse? Nobody's ever made me so curious in my life.'

'And?' said Arapera and fixed him with a look. 'Would you please get to it before I expire?'

'He said, he fell for Linda the first time he met her at the dentist, she was the receptionist there. He asked her out and they went out for drinks and dinner a few times and then he wanted to take her to bed - and she refused.'

Jackson started to laugh, half amused and half

embarrassed. 'For God's sake, please don't go into details about my mum's love life. I can't take it!'

'There won't be any details,' said Liam. 'That was just setting the scene. So Linda said they could never have a real relationship however much she liked him because ten years down the track the age difference would embarrass him, and if it didn't embarrass him it would embarrass her! Because he had made it clear he wanted it to be long-term.'

'Wow!' said Carter on a note of surprise. 'Fancy turning someone like him down? I mean, he's very attractive, gorgeous actually.'

'And now they're engaged,' said Arapera. 'And mum looks fifteen years younger or nearly, so how did that happen?'

'I'll quote his exact words,' said Liam and she could see the grin lurking at the corner of his mouth and suddenly felt like kissing him. 'He told her he wasn't worried, but if she was concerned it was easily fixed, but he needed her for her energy and her smile. He sent her off to Dunedin's top plastic surgeon and then to a private lodge cum spa somewhere down near Queenstown for a month and she came back transformed and they're both very happy.'

'Aha,' said Carter and raised his glass. 'Hence the suddenly ten years younger face and the slim body and the hair! Great move, Linda!'

'Apparently it wasn't easy.' Liam smiled at Arapera, who was trying to come to terms with what he had just told her, such a surprising story. 'It took four months for him to persuade her that to do it at all, and then she got the admin job at the winery when she returned, and now she's doing their online promotions and social media too, and they've hired another admin woman. And he's not as young as he looks, he's nearly my age.'

Jackson whistled under his breath. 'Epic!'

'But why did he say to do or say whatever mum asked us? I don't get it. She didn't actually ask me anything.' Arapera thinks for a moment then adds, 'But we weren't alone at all, not for five seconds. She has so many friends now – she never did before. It's unreal – this change and how she seems like a different person. I wonder if Juan knows about our past, how hard it was and how it worked out … for me.'

She saw Carter's look at Liam and wondered if he was worried about what might come out now, on the day of surprises.

'I've no idea. He didn't say anything about it, and I didn't ask.' Liam looked steadily at Arapera. 'The past did happen, but it's your and Linda's reality. I wouldn't think she would tell him any details, and maybe she doesn't even admit to herself that she let you down so badly.'

'Shit no!' said Jackson. 'She might say her marriage was bad, or she was married to a terrible man, but would she say how she couldn't protect her own daughter? No way!'

Carter interjected mildly, 'But she did leave him,

Jackson, and she did take you to live in another town. That counts for something, I think. Even it was for her own benefit, it did help you, Arapera. And, of course, you got to know me, which was a fringe benefit so to speak, but must count for something.'

Liam held his glass up in a mock toast. 'The incredible Juan thought Linda might ask you not to tell people your ages or something like it – it seems she's been quite nervous about it. Because Linda thinks his parents don't know her real age and she doesn't want them to.' And then he laughed. 'But Juan thinks his parents have known nearly from the start, at least his mother, who said something once, just after Linda started working there – but they've never discussed it.'

'Like some romantic novel,' said Jackson and yawned. 'One of those you mentioned, sis – the ones with a bare-chested hero on the cover. This one's probably called Love among the vines or something.'

Chapter 43

A couple of days later Arapera put her phone down and looked across at Liam. 'One hundred and four! She's bought one hundred and four things, and now she's going to have to get a freight company to pack them in a big crate and ship them back.'

'Are you talking about Fiona?' Liam looked up from the list he was reading. 'Hey, what does sm/cup mean – is it something to do with underwear or what? I'm trying to figure out if everything on your list will fit in the car or if we need to do two trips.'

Arapera walked across to the table to see what he is looking at. 'What? Underwear? Oh, that's not a bra, Liam, don't be silly, it's short for small cupboard. It's the only thing bigger than clothes and some towels and my secret wine supply that I'm bringing back. It's a gorgeous little cabinet I have in my bedroom that I bought in an op-shop last year. It fits in a corner, and it has a curved door and it's made from birds-eye maple – I thought it might be nice in the corner of the guest room. It will fit in the back if we fold the backseat down. We can't fit any other furniture in here, the rest of my stuff can stay in the flat, and when Carter finds a flatmate, they'll have to sort it out.'

'Tell me what Fiona said – I interrupted you. She's bought loads of stuff?'

'Yeah, she says it will keep us busy for weeks, she's never bought so much before. She went back to that place I told you about, the place she was at when she called me before we went away. The owners were delighted with how much she bought, and she's delighted with her finds, but some are heavy and quite large. And she's got a Lalique vase that she insisted on paying them treble the price for because they had no idea what it was – she didn't tell them, but she says it will sell for a hundred times that when it's been cleaned up.'

'OK, let's go tomorrow afternoon and stay on to have that dinner you said Carter offered us if we come this week.'

'These things that have happened lately, they have changed everything,' said Arapera that night and looked at Liam's face which somehow always seemed most familiar when they were lying down, like a lasting first impression from the accident scene, the confirmation of who he was and why he mattered so much. 'I want to tell you about it, but it's hard to describe.'

She wanted to explain to him how dramatic this change was, how she felt it created a different future for her, but it was hard to think of a way to describe it for Liam to understand it the way she felt it. Perhaps, she thought, she could liken it to feeling as if before she had no substance, because the things that she held close to her heart were not seen by others. That what had kept her going and acting normal was the knowledge that she was strong and that her father could not cow her spirit, that she survived and coped and refused to be diminished by his abuse. But others didn't know what went on behind the scenes and what she coped with, so for them the quality she treasured most in herself was not obvious. She was silent for a long time, looking inward and trying to find the words to express what she felt was important for Liam to understand.

'When I was a teenager, I felt as if I cast no shadow,' she said finally, grateful that Liam had not felt the need to fill the silence, just waited patiently. 'It was as if I had no substance in the eyes of the world because nobody knew how strong I was. Perhaps if I had told Jackson or auntie Jean, it would have been different, but I never told anyone apart from Carter after we had moved with my mother to Levin. I got to know Carter at the end of the school year, but I didn't tell him then, not until we were a couple of years older, and he asked me about the scars on my back when I went swimming without my T-shirt on. Some of the netball girls had noticed too but I said I'd been trapped in a barbed wire fence when I was little.'

She paused and thought for a moment and Liam watched her without comment until

she continued. 'But now I don't feel like that —it's gone, completely gone. I only just realised that night at the engagement party when I was watching mum dancing. I can't forgive her for not helping me, but I can separate who she is now from who she was then. I can't forgive dad and I never will, but he no longer has the power to terrify me. It's not that I can forget what happened, I can remember all the details, of course — how could I not? But it doesn't do anything to me. I don't feel that I would cry if I had to tell someone about it.'

Liam remained silent, as if he could sense that there was more to come, and she reached out and put her hand on his cheek. 'This is how different it is now,' she said seriously. 'It's as if something that's been playing like a video clip in my mind all these years, has turned into a photo — it's not alive now, it's a still image. I don't have to relive it - I can look at it as a memory.'

'And you still don't want your father prosecuted?'

'Oh no,' she said quietly. 'It's pointless, isn't it? It would do nothing for me, just bring me once again into the spotlight, even if it's only in a court room. And now that he might be getting treatment it seems pointless - punishment would do him no good. As far as we know he's never attacked anyone outside the family – there are no unacknowledged victims out there.'

'How Carter handled him was amazing when I think back on it.' Liam smiled at the memory. 'I went over to intercept Jackson to prevent him from intervening when I spotted him arriving, but I watched Carter the whole the time – a calm, lowkey approach and somehow, he managed to deal with it without a manic outburst, a marvellous skill. I bet he's a real asset as an ED nurse.'

Arapera smiled. 'It's his size too – I think the combination of how calm and softspoken he is, and his size - that's the magic formula that makes people trust him. They probably don't expect it and it gives them pause.' And then she laughed and added. 'And you've got no idea how much that combination appeals to women, they love him! He's had flocks of them after him for years – and then they get so disappointed when discover he's gay.'

She woke in the middle of the night, turned under Liam's arm so she could feel him against her back and his words from that first night in his bed flashed back into her mind. 'Am I your rock to stand on?' and she smiled, closed her eyes and went back to sleep.

Letters from the Past

Letters from the Past is a series of stand-alone novels where a letter from or about the past reveals something that changes a woman's perceptions of herself or of her family, and that affects her outlook on life.

These books are such fun to write, and I am always working on the next title in this series. I hope you will enjoy reading them as much as I enjoy writing them!

Tina

Having had nobody in her life since her husband died, Lara unexpectedly finds herself involved with three men. One is planning to use her, one she plans to use for her own ends, and one becomes a "friend-with-benefits" with surprising results. Sometimes a quiet schoolteacher is not all she seems at first glance.

Callista experiences an event of apparent ESP at the Okehampton Castle ruins and becomes a media sensation, but the effect it has on her life is dramatic. How do two people, one calm. one seriously claustrophobic, who feel they are poles apart, cope for an hour and a half in total darkness in a stalled lift? And can they handle the consequences?

Sofia's life is in turmoil: a difficult diva mother, a letter with a confession about a family killing and having to accept help from a man she loathes when she is injured. Can reluctant attraction turn into love?

Who is the stranger living in the empty house Miranda inherited from her grandmother? Why is he living like a secretive recluse in someone else's house? Reckless Miranda decides to confront him, and what she discovers prompts her to set out on a fearless quest to bring justice to a man who has given up hope. But is the gamble too great or a risk worth taking?

When Emma finds an old letter in a library book she is instantly intrigued, but by researching the origin of the letter she unwittingly opens the door to danger and becomes the target for threats and harassment. Nearly desperate, she takes a leap of blind faith into the unknown and accepts an offer of help from a stranger - but can she trust him?

Jamie, an ardent protester against the gigantic Vista Resort development and Leo Masters, the high-powered developer, seem unlikely to ever agree on anything. But unexpected coincidences and chance brings them together in a fragile state of mutual respect. Will courage and kindness resolve the situation, or do they need help?

After a bizarre accident with ESP overtones, the media haunt Arapera. But can she trust an offer of help from a man she has only met once? Or will she regret it for the rest of her life if she doesn't take the chance? Sometimes life is a knife-edge balance between staying safe and taking risks, and there is no way of predicting if the gamble is worth it.

RUNNING TOWARD DANGER

Also by Tina Clough

THE GIRL WHO LIVED TWICE

What would you do if you woke up one morning and found that time had rewound exactly a year? Would you revisit your past mistakes and try to do better? Would you try to get revenge on those who had wronged you? Or would you use what you knew to get rich? When Mia finds herself in her own past, she must decide how best to use her pre-knowledge of one year's worth of events and personal issues.

RUNNING TOWARDS DANGER

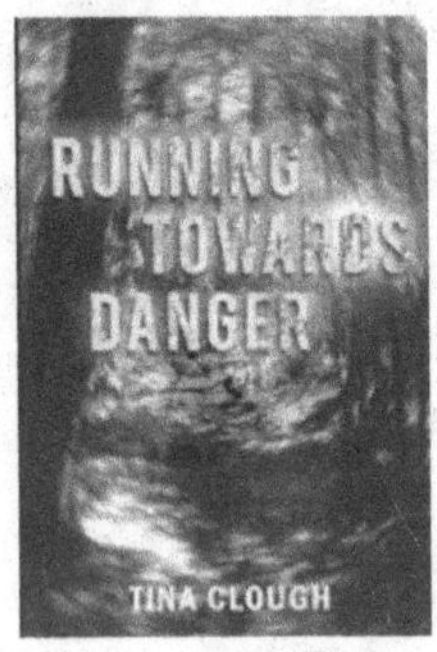

When Karen's flat-mate Nick is gunned down in front of her in the street her life is turned upside-down. Everything she thought she knew about him turns out to be a lie. She becomes a suspect in the police investigation and drug bosses think she knows where Nick has hidden a large sum of money. When her life is threatened, she decides to leave town and disappear.

Karen becomes Cara and creates an anonymous existence, severs all links to her past and adopts a cash-based way of life that leaves no electronic traces. But despite her careful planning danger still stalks her and she is forced to make dramatic choices in the face of threats and brutal violence.

Can she trust the man she is attracted to, or has he been sent by the killers to gain her confidence and find the money they believe she has?

THE CHINESE PROVERB

Book 1 - Hunter Grant Series

Army veteran Hunter Grant thought he had left war behind in Afghanistan – a conflict that left him with physical and psychological scars.

But finding an unconscious girl in the Northland bush and gradually untangling her story involves him in warfare of a different kind in his own country.

Hunter sets out to find and punish the man Dao calls Master, but he soon finds there is more to this story than enslavement. Before long he himself is being hunted by the overlord of a drug empire whose sole objective is to kill Dao because she knows too much.

Protecting her and waging war while trying to keep the police from stifling his enterprise takes all Hunter's ingenuity and determination and puts him in deadly jeopardy.

ONE SINGLE THING

Book 2 - Hunter Grant Series

Journalist Hope Barber disappears two weeks after returning to New Zealand from an assignment in Pakistan, leaving her front door open and her bag and phone inside. The police are tight-lipped about their reluctance to act, and Hunter Grant and Dao agree to help Hope's brother Noah find her. Details about Hope's time in Pakistan gradually emerge but only raise more questions.

Was Hope under surveillance?

Was she linked to terrorists?

And who is the man Hope called 'my stalker'?

FOLDED

Book 3 - Hunter Grant Series

First notes asking for help and folded into tiny origami shapes are found outside a city apartment building, then a physics textbook with tiny writing between the lines and then the woman who found them abruptly resigns and disappears. Are the notes asking for help real or is it a game? Hunter Grant, ex-army and with a pragmatic view of justice, reluctantly agrees to help find the missing woman.

Things get complicated when a high-powered lawyer arrives form the US, and shortly after his meeting with Hunter and Dao, a "cease and desist" letter arrives from the Cayman Islands. Inspector Bakker - a woman, who in Hunter's words "looks as if she would be useful in a brawl, provided she was on your side" - takes instant exception to his involvement and threatens to arrest him for interfering in an investigation.

Dao sets out alone on a dangerous mission, driven by a compulsive need to find out what has happened to the girl who wrote the notes, and Hunter looks death in the face when he decides to risk everything to put an end to the Darknet forces that threaten their lives.

THE SHADOW BROKER

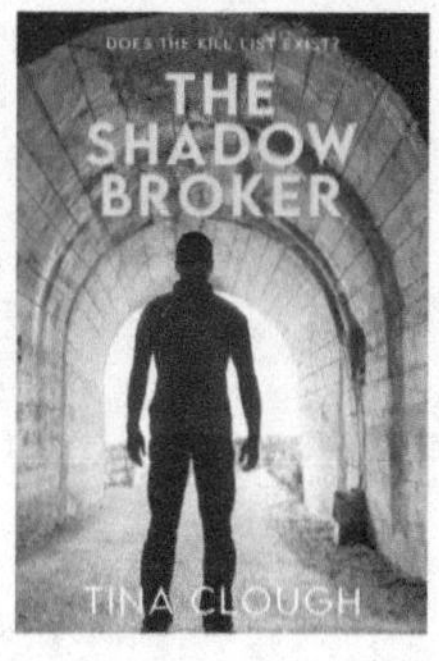

It is 2026 and individual freedoms are severely curtailed, with state surveillance everywhere. State Security has a Watch List, and being on it means that nothing you do or say escapes the authorities, but does the Kill List really exist? And if it does, how would you know if you were on it?

Coded messages on a found burner phone, top-level government corruption and a shadowy mastermind who calls himself The Broker. In this climate of state control, three unlikely friends start quietly looking for connections and set in motion a deadly game of hide and seek that will change their lives forever.

Trying to uncover the truth means risking your life, and nothing is more dangerous than searching for evidence of government corruption.

About the Author

Tina Clough grew up in Sweden and now lives in New Zealand; dividing her time between writing fiction and translating and editing medical research papers.

Between working and writing she looks after an acre of fruit trees, vegetable gardens and roaming hens.

Apart from reading her interests include photography, wine, growing organic vegetables, making jam and kayaking.

https://lightpoolpublishing.com